MERCY

QUEEN'S BIRDS OF PREY BOOK 1

KATHI S. BARTON

World Castle Publishing, LLC
Pensacola, Florida
Copyright © Kathi S. Barton 2019
Paperback ISBN: 9781949812589
eBook ISBN: 9781949812596
First Edition World Castle Publishing, LLC, January 7, 2019
http://www.worldcastlepublishing.com
Licensing Notes
Cover: Karen Fuller
Editor: Maxine Bringenberg

Prologue

The castle was going down, thanks wholly to her birds. Queen Dante sat upon her horse and watched as stone after stone crumbled to the ground. In a matter of moments, not only were the walls to the fort destroyed, but the king inside his castle was dead as well. Turning her mount, she headed back to the encampment to ready herself for the long ride home. The birds joined her not half an hour later, their large bodies covered in dust and blood.

"You have done well, my darlings." They could understand her and she them, but no one else could. She had made them what they were, and she would be the only one to control them. "Have you fed well on his dying cattle? How does it serve a man to have his food dying? His people, they were fed no better, I saw."

The birds—she had never named them—told her that the people were headed west. In a few months, maybe less, they would all be dead too. It bothered them when the people suffered because of the king or queen of the castle. But it was to be. Dante could not care for any more in her own keep.

5

No one would attack her keep. If they tried, she knew them to be too stupid or too drunk on their own mead. She had her birds, all of them bigger than life, made large by magic that she gave them. Looking at them as they landed around her, forever keeping her safe, she wondered why she had not thought of it sooner, when her king was still alive.

"I would have set you upon him. You could have eaten him for your dinner. Though I suspect that it would have given you a great deal of belly pains." The hawk told her that she was lucky that he had died the way he had. No one would come for her if she had killed him. "Yes, that is very true. But I suffered greatly when he was living. No children with me to give me comfort in my olden age. Though they might have been just like him, and that would have been too much to bear."

She would never marry again. Love wasn't something that she searched for. Not that she didn't have someone to warm her bed on occasion, but it was nice to be able to send them on their way when she was finished with them. Her heart belonged to no one, and she would not take another man to her bed by force. All would be well, and no one would threaten to come and take over her home, she hoped. The birds' as well.

The hawk used her beak to put delicate things upon the backs of the others. There was aplenty this time. Barrels and smoked meats. Pottery that they would use like it wasn't worth a king's gold. They raided the castle each time they conquered. Hawk was the best at getting in and out before they took the places to the ground.

The eagle took off toward home. She would let the people know that the queen was returning simply by her showing up. They would have a feast this night. The food upon her back would feed them for many days, and the barrels of spices that had been hoarded in the lower levels of the king's castle would go a long way toward trading what they did not grow.

The phoenix, by far the most deadly of her birds, shed her feathers in anticipation of getting new ones. After a battle she would become anew, each time getting stronger, and her feathers, brilliant now, would be brighter still. She could flame a fire so hot that stone would crumble under a man's feet. The ground would no longer hold a seed within its belly to produce food, and she could kill a man with a single breath so that there would be nothing left of his body.

Dante loaded the last of her things onto the back of the owl. She might be small, she had always thought, but she could carry more than her own weight. And she would pick up her horse, used to flying through the sky like a bird himself, and take him back to the castle. He would be fed and groomed before Dante ever landed on the ground.

The vulture squawked at her, and she turned to look at the two men there. They looked as if they might have been about to kill her, but the sight of such large birds threw them off their duty. In no time at all the vulture snapped both of them up and ate them. A gruesome sight, but one that filled her heart with joy too. She was safe again. The vulture took off once she was loaded up.

"Well, my falcon, it is just you and I left." She told her that she was still armed. "Yes, well, probably not too bad of an idea seeing that they nearly shot us."

The falcon laid her body to the ground. She was the only one that was fitted with a seat, one that Dante rode on. Scouring the area, Dante always made sure that she left the places that she camped as neat and clean as she'd found them. Sometimes in better shape. As she climbed onto the back of her bird, she held her breath.

"I do hate the height. I should have thought this through

when I turned you into my warriors." Her laughter, should there have been someone around to hear it, might have sounded insane. "Homeward, my love, and we shall eat well tonight."

She took no one with her on her fights, except the birds. That was why, she believed, her people were so loyal to her— she protected them. Fed them better than herself and made sure that there was plenty for them to trade and share for things that she did not provide for them.

The soil was rich and would give forth a bounty like no other gardens. Flowers that were woven into pretty things and traded. There was a smithy, as well as a doctor who doubled as a dentist. They had even acquired a grave digger, who doubled as a man who made markers.

A single merchant that came by, his wagon filled when he arrived, would leave with the wagon near empty. He would bring the latest news with him, and any posts that he had been asked to bring to them. He would also, for a small coin, take out posts for the next time he was in the keep of a relative or friend.

And today there was such a missive, but it was for her, from someone that she had hoped never to hear from again. The king of the land—the only man that she answered to, though it wasn't with any kind of happiness on her part.

After the others were settled down and the food that had been brought put into storage, she sat down and wasn't surprised that the falcon came to see her. The room that she was in—the throne room, for lack of a better term—had no roof, and six perches for the birds when they wished to see her. Otherwise they sat upon the top of the castle turrets, watching for anything that might befall them.

"I am to wed. The king of the land, he has decided that my castle, Duncan Castle, is the best there is, and he will marry

8

me himself." They asked about his castle. "He says that it will be his son's, which he has none as yet. His last five wives only gave him daughters, from what I have heard, and they did not last long afterwards."

The falcon asked her what she would do. Dante knew what would happen to her should he come here. He would kill her. Being in her fortieth summer, she was much too old to bear children now, and he would be better with a younger bride. One that could birth him the sons that he wanted.

"He will kill me, we all know that. And you six will kill him or be killed. I worry so much for the people here too." She thought of several plans and threw them out. It was in her head that if she should die, then she would do so on her own terms. "I will need a day to think on this. In the meantime, he says that he will be here in the new year. That will give us a month to provide for the people and make sure that they are not harmed."

To be continued in book two, Hawk.

Chapter 1

Mercy was pissed, which if she thought about it, was a normality for her. But today she thought she had a good reason to be. The people that worked for her were not doing what she wanted. Before she could go down to the floor and tear into a few of them, Blaze joined her in her office.

"They say that it might rain today." Mercy sat down, waiting for Blaze to get to her point. If she had one. "I was thinking that later today, while it's storming, we could go on a long flight. It'll do us both, mostly you, some good to get out and be yourself for a while."

"We're behind in production, and you want to take to the skies like it's nothing at all." Blaze smiled and nodded. "This is not the time, nor am I in the mood, for you to be your sweet self. I'm mad."

"You are forever mad, Mercy. I think you should have picked a better name than Mercy, because you certainly don't seem to have much. Maybe you should have picked Bullheaded. Or Asshole. That's the favorite among the ones that work for you." Mercy asked her if that was true. "It is. I'd

11

not lie to you about this, even if I could. But you're not only too hard on yourself, but on everyone around you. Including us. And you have been since the day our queen passed."

"She was the only person that I ever loved besides the other birds like me." Blaze said that she knew that. "I miss her every day. And it's been eons since we were changed, yet I hate it just the same as the day it happened."

"Because you have never been free, Mercy. All you have done since then was to try and figure out a way for you to make us coin...money. And you know that we have more than enough to live out the rest of our days without a need for any more. The bounty that was left for us was more than ample, yet you still strive to make more." That was true, but when one told you that you would never die, it made a person—her—terrified of being without a place to hide, food, and something to do every boring day. "What would you do today if you weren't at work? And I want you to realize that today is Saturday, when most of these people working for you would rather be home and spending time with their families."

"I don't know. Working is all I know how to do." Blaze leaned back in her chair, as if she had just come up with the formula for some ancient remedy. "What do you propose I do, Blaze? I haven't any idea what taking a day off means. And you might be right about the people that work for me. My turnover rate is higher this month."

"Because it's summer and kids are home from school. People are taking vacations and working at making time for their children. Not for their asshole of a boss who makes them work overtime. Even though there is a great deal of product ready to go out at a moment's notice."

Mercy flushed. She did have enough of the little tin toys to go out. Lucky for her she'd had some of the ones that she'd seen in stores ages ago, and when she saw a need for them again. it was easy enough to start production on them since she had some of the originals. With just a small change here and there, she had a viable product to sell.

"Here is what I'm going to do for you, Mercy. I'm going to book you a vacation and you will take it. Without your cell phone, without any kind of computer or tablet. And you will enjoy yourself." Mercy opened her mouth to protest. She was a grown woman, damn it. "You have to do this. If you don't, you're going to be the most hated boss and friend that has ever been made."

When Blaze left her to tell her employees they were going to close the plant for two weeks and that they'd be paid for it, Mercy sat in her office trying to think why she was going to do this. She knew that she'd been working too hard, and that her stress level was through the roof. But the need to have reserves, of everything, had followed her throughout her entire human life.

Being changed into what she was hadn't been anything that she wanted. When the queen had told them of her plan, she never mentioned that they'd be around forever. Nor did she tell them that with their change, that they'd be able to be both sizes of birds. The smaller one that could take flight whenever they wanted. And the larger one that could be destructive as well as keep them safe—the large predators that helped save an entire kingdom.

Leaning back in her chair, she closed her eyes. Mercy tried very hard not to remember the events of that time, and today was no different. But her heart hurt for the woman that had given her life so that they might have theirs. Not that Mercy cared for her life, but she was going to make the most of it for Dante. Exhaustion took her under in just a matter of seconds.

The nap had done her a world of good, and she was ready

to face the rest of her day. Opening her computer, she saw four messages from Blaze, as well as two from Esme. Mercy opened Esmeralda's first. She was always a good one to have a laugh with.

I hear that you're going on a trip. Yay! I'd like to say that I want you to have fun, but we both know that not only will you be worrying about your business, but also looking for a new project to get going. I love you, Mercy, so please, get laid. Have a one-night stand, and for all the love in the world, try and rest. You're beginning to look your age.

With a happy face, Mercy signed off.

After making sure that all her emails were taken care of, she put in a note saying that she was going on a vacation. It took her ten minutes of trying to decide if she needed to do this when Blaze emailed her again.

Her plans were set. All she had to do was go to the airport. There wasn't any mention of where she was going or what she was doing, but she figured that once she got it, if it didn't suit her, she'd just go where she wanted.

Mercy didn't need to pack much in the way of clothing — just something for show, as well as any kind of personal items that she would need. Not having to buy clothing — or for that matter, wash anything — had been given to them by Dante as well. They each had the ability to wear whatever they wanted at any time just by thinking about it.

The airport was crowded when she arrived. Blaze had told her that she was leaving tonight and would be able to enjoy her holiday in the morning. Mercy had no idea how she thought that was going to work. She didn't even want to go on this thing. But there was a plane on the tarmac just for her to use. Blaze, apparently, had gone all out for this thing.

The plane was much nicer than she had remembered. They owned a fleet of planes that would deliver their merchandise all over the world. Not only did Mercy produce tin toys but Blaze designed clothing that was in all the big-name stores and online.

Jude handled all the online orders for both their businesses, which was very lucrative. Most of the sales for both of their business was from that very way of buying. The catalog that had been put there had special things that could only be purchased online.

Piper worked with metals, making the most incredible art with her own flame. Things that people who wanted a handmade proclamation that they had money would hang on their homes. Nothing she did was cheap.

Remi had a string of restaurants all over the world. She didn't work in any of them, but she could cook a meal that would make even the best chef jealous. And after they all approved of the meal, or gave their comments on it, she would then perfect it and put it on the menu. Her restaurants were featured in news writeups that gave her rave reviews.

Esme was an artist. That sounded so lame for what she did. Not only did she work with paints and canvas, but she had taken to making the finest jewelry that Mercy had ever seen. In fact, Mercy thought, she was wearing a piece of her work now. It was a pretty bracelet that had each of their birds on it. And their eyes on the bracelet were the colors of the castle they had been to with the Queen Dante and destroyed.

The plane took off on time and Mercy was brought a glass of wine. She so loved the taste of the white grapes that she'd bought herself a vineyard to make sure that the one that she enjoyed most never went out of business. The people that ran it were doing a good job, and sales for that were very nice too.

Mercy wondered if she was headed to a fat farm. Not that she'd need that — none of them could gain an ounce except for being with child. Mercy knew that wouldn't happen to her.

15

She wasn't the type of person that men fawned all over. She wasn't very tolerant of men in general.

It wasn't as if she felt like her life was ruined by being what she was, but her life had been taken from her—at least the one that she had wanted to live. As she'd been born a falcon, she had thought that she'd live a full life—the one before the magic had changed her—and then die.

Dante had told them of the king's decree that she wed him. Dante had also known that he was only doing it to take her castle. They all figured that the wedding night would be the last night alive for the queen of the castle, for he would surely kill her for someone much younger to bear him a boy child.

"Miss? The plane is about to land. May I get you anything before we do?" She asked her where they were. "I'm not supposed to tell you, but I'd dig out some shorts if I were you. I think it's in the mid-nineties today."

She'd sent her someplace hot? It would be like Blaze to make the next stop on this trip someplace where it was in the mid-nineties below zero. Getting up when the plane touched down, Mercy went to one of the little windows and looked out.

There wasn't much to see but the airport. There might have been palm trees, but it was moving by so quickly that she didn't have time to make it out. The plane she was on came to a smooth stop when it got to its gate, and Mercy decided that she'd know more about this trip if she would just get off the damned plane.

Mercy had to catch herself from snarling at everyone. Twice now she'd had to count to ten before asking as politely as one could through clenched teeth where she was. It was hot. As soon as she stepped off the plane it had slapped her no less hard than a good punch to the mouth. But she was here,

16

and and it looked like she wasn't ever going to enjoy herself.

Hearing her name called over the intercom, she looked around for a white courtesy phone. When she finally located one, not only was it not working, but it had gum all over the handle and now all over her hand. Christ, this was one of the biggest mistakes she'd ever made.

Finally locating a phone that worked, she wasn't in a great mood. And no matter how many times she counted to fifty, nothing was working to sooth her temper. The man at the other end did not help his cause when he answered her return call with laughter.

"Look buddy. I've had the worse ten minutes anyone could endure. I'm supposed to be on a fucking vacation, not running all over the airport looking for a phone so you could blow me off by thinking this is some sort of joke. What the fuck do you want?" He laughed again. "I don't know what you want, but as of his moment, I'm going to murder you."

"Blaze said that you'd not be in the best of humor when I picked you up. I'm the man near the limo that is waiting for you to come out so that we can be on this adventure." She asked him what the limo was for. "To convey a person or persons from one point to the next. With all your smarts, as I've been told you have, I'd think you'd know that much."

With a growl she hung up on the man. Making her way to the front of the airport, she tried to cool her temper, to no avail. Stomping across the room, noticing that people were jumping out of her way, Mercy felt slightly sick to her stomach. Her head was pounding as well. And when she saw the man standing at a long white limo, it was all she could do to stand upright. Stopping quickly did not help her, and Mercy knew that she was going down.

~*~

Joel had never seen a woman go down like that before.

17

And had he not been there to catch her, he was sure that she would have knocked her head on the stones around the sidewalk, and then the people around her would have picked her body clean of anything that she had.

Glancing over at her as she lay on the gurney with a wet cool towel on her head, he wondered about her. She was gorgeous, he could see that, and her vile temper that Blaze had told him about didn't seem to be all that bad. Of course, he'd only spoken to her on the phone once. She might be worse than he'd been told.

Joel stretched out his long legs and laid his head back to rest. Working four jobs, all of them part-time, was paying his and his daughter's bills, but it wasn't giving them anything extra. But this gig was going to put them in the black for the first time since his daughter was born.

Having one full time job with benefits, as well as a part-time one so he could use the extra money for school trips for Miley, would be wonderful. And to be able to afford bandages and the smelly stuff that he used on her cuts would be just fine with him. Smiling, he thought of Miley just this morning when she'd taken a tumble down the wet stairs.

"I hurt myself again, Daddy. And if you think that I'm going to let you paint me up with that stuff, you can just forget it. It's a cut. I'm fine. I'm pretty sure that I'm not going to lose my leg over it." He cocked his brow at her. "And don't do that. You know that it makes you look like Grandda. And you said that he never had a lick of sense to get in out of the rain."

"Who the fuck are you?" He looked at the young woman next to him. "Better yet, where the hell am I? Did you kidnap me?"

"Yes, that's why I announced to anyone around that I was picking you up. Just to whisk you away to the hospital." She glared. "Ms. Dante, I have a thirteen-year-old daughter.

18

You could learn the glaring from her. Now, you fainted. And I caught you before you did some real damage or were left unattended. Didn't you eat on the plane?"

"I didn't know where I was going, so no, I did not eat on the plane." He asked her what one had to do with the other. "Just go away and leave me alone. I've had enough of this vacation shit. I'm going back home to work. It was easier to deal with."

"You can't do that. Well, I suppose you could, but I'd rather you didn't. I have a lot depending on this job for Blaze, and I sure could use the money." She told him that she'd give it to him. "No, that won't work either. I'm not a man that takes handouts. I have to work to earn my keep."

"But you'll take it from her for being a fucking pain in the ass to me?" He nodded and grinned at her. "You are certifiable. Where am I?"

"It's called the Island Hospital, but most around here call it Death Valley. Once you check in, mostly you never check out. Not that they'd kill you off, but you, a woman that looks like she has money and more than likely insurance, they'll keep you until the insurance runs out or you die. Test after test would be taken. They might even try and remove something you need just to get some more money."

"And you brought me here." He said that the ambulance had, and he figured that she'd rather be here than at his home. "Yes, you're right. But I want you to know that I'm not a push over."

"I know that. Blaze described you well enough that I'd know you anywhere. Did you really call the president of the United States and tell him to fuck off when you were told that you couldn't buy an army issued Humvee?" She nodded like she would do it again if necessary. "I guess you didn't get your car."

"On the contrary. He was very accommodating when I pointed out that I will move all my businesses to another country, and not pay the taxes that he was imposing on me. I will pay them, but I won't be cheated." She stood up, and he held her by the arms until she no longer swayed. "I have to get something to eat. Where is the closest restaurant?"

"Closed. Not that I'd recommend you eat there anyway, but you didn't ask where a clean one was." Mercy asked if he was serious. "Yes, my daughter, Miley, she's forever telling me I have to learn to fib better to customers. I can't do that and live with myself. She's a good kid."

"I'm sure that she's wonderful. Where might I get something to eat that isn't going to have me ending up back here?" He thought of his home and the roast he'd put on this morning in anticipation of the money coming in. "Where is that head of yours?"

"I don't think you're going to like it, but you are more than welcome to come to my house. My little girl is there, and she can act as a chaperone for us if that would bother you." She tisked at him. "Or, I can take you to your hotel, and you can try and convince them that you are a wealthy person and demand a steak dinner. That might work, but I'd be careful of spit in my food."

"Your daughter is correct, you do need to fib better. Or at the very least honey coat your responses before you say them. Your house it is, then." Joel was still standing there when she moved out of the curtained area. "Are you coming or not? Since I can't drive, nor do I know where you live, I need you to get your ass in gear and come on."

Smiling, Joel followed. Miley was going to have a shit fit when they turned up. He thought about calling her to give her a heads up, but was afraid that she'd run off. Not that she'd ever done that before, but he didn't bring home women

20

either. Nearly skipping to the limo that was still there, he opened the door for Mercy.

"What's your name? I mean, if you plan to kill me off or something—which I must warn you isn't going to happen—then I'd like to be able to tell the police who it is that I had to murder to save my own life." He told her that she was very sure of herself. "Oh, you have no idea. None at all."

She looked around then back at him. And her hair—Christ, her hair turned into feathers and ran down along her back to her legs. Then, just as suddenly, she turned back to her normal beautiful self. Joel had no idea how long he stood there. His mouth, he knew was hanging open. Snapping it shut, he got in on the other side of the limo.

Drive, his mind told him, and he started the big car up. Laughter from the backseat, soft and sexy, made his cock stretch and his mind dip into fantasies that he'd never had before. Silky sheets, sweaty bodies, and loud and soft moans. At the next light, he laid his head on the steering wheel.

"Are you all right?" He told her that he wasn't. "I'm sorry. I didn't mean to freak you out with my shift. It's just that I was trying to piss you off. What's wrong?"

"I...nothing. I'm going to call my daughter and tell her we're having company. Can you please not do that hair thing around her?" Mercy said that she'd not. "My name is Joel Oliver. My daughter is Miley Oliver. We're not rich, as you'll see, and we don't put on airs that we're something that we're not. So, I'm asking—no, I'm telling you to behave yourself. Or you'll find yourself without a driver or dinner. All right?"

"Yes."

She didn't say anything the rest of the way to his house. He supposed he could have been nicer, but he wasn't going to have his little girl traumatized any more than she already had been.

21

Joel thought about how his daughter had come to him. When he'd been younger and much broker than he was now, he had sold his sperm. It didn't pay that well, but it was enough for him to eat a good meal at a fast food restaurant, as well as put gas in his car. He'd sold blood too, as he was a rare type, and that had paid better but not great. Joel had been broke since he'd been a child.

The children's services of Oklahoma had called him, telling him that his child had been in a car accident, and asked if he was willing to come and get her. He hadn't any idea what they were talking about, and after an attorney showed up on his doorstep, he realized that a woman had used his donation and had Miley.

"The mother is...I don't know how to tell you this, sir, but the company that she got your donation from was less than stellar. They should never have given— But that isn't important. The woman in question was very intoxicated and ran a red light. It wasn't the first time that she'd done such a thing. But this time it ended tragically, for both her and the little girl. We don't normally do this sort of thing, contact someone that has helped in this sort of situation, but I don't want to see this brilliant little girl go into the system." Right then, without any kind of knowledge about Miley, he said that he'd take her. "Good. There will be money coming in from the company that dealt with the woman, and that will come to you in the form of a check monthly."

He decided then to put the money in an account for Miley to use for college. It wasn't as if he couldn't have used the money—there were times when it was tempting as hell to dip into it. But Joel only had to look into the face of his daughter to know that the money would do more for her future than for him to not have to walk to work a few times a week. He pushed the button on the steering wheel to call his daughter.

Joel loved modern techs.

"Dad, you're not going to believe this. I have to write a report on ancient times. Like that is going to help me when I get out of school. I can see it now—I'll be on a date and he'll only want to talk about stuff that happened well before either of us were even thought of, much less our parents. Why are you calling me?" Laughing, he told her that they were going to have a guest for dinner. "Oh really? A woman guest? Should I change the sheets on your bed?"

"Miley Ann. My goodness, the stuff that comes out of your mouth sometimes. No, you do not go in my room again. The last time you tidied up, it took me a week to find my shoes." He laughed with her. "No, she's the lady that I was going to ride around all week. Be nice."

"I'm always nice to strangers. It's you that I have to be snarky to." The laughter from the back had him realizing that Mercy could hear every word they were saying. "But I will peel some potatoes and bake one of those long breads that you like. Oh, and the mail has some things in it you have to deal with. Dad, I need to help out around here."

"We'll talk about it later. But for now, just make sure that the trash is taken out and you vacuum. Miss Dante and I will be there shortly." Past due notices. "Also, I'll see about helping you with your homework when I get there."

After closing the connection, he glanced in the mirror. Mercy was still sitting staring out the window, but he had a feeling that she could have told him every word he and Miley had said. He would only be driving her this week, he told himself, and after that, he'd never see her again. The money was just too good to stop now.

Chapter 2

Mercy, what do you care if he's asked you to behave. You can be a bit caustic when it suits you. She couldn't argue with Piper about that—she was. But Mercy wanted Piper to tell her it would be all right to kill the man. *You haven't done any kind of research on this man, so I'll tell you. This guy is one day, I think, from losing it all. He's having trouble meeting his house payment, his car is about as old as he is, and he has a little girl that has issues as well. The car accident that killed her mother left her paralyzed from the waist down. And she rides around in an older wheelchair because they cannot afford to get her another one. This money that he's being paid to carry you around is going to be the difference between him sleeping in that old car or having his house payment brought up to date.*

Mercy wanted to say that wasn't any of her concern, that she'd not hired the jerk, but didn't. The conversation that she'd overheard between him and his daughter was light, funny, and full of love. Nothing that she'd experienced since Dante had died.

I think I'm coming home. Piper said that if she did, then all of them were leaving her alone for a year. *No, that won't work for me. I demand that you allow me to come home. I'll pay the man for his job. I don't like this shit.*

Tough. You will stay on that vacation or I will come there and beat the shit out of you. You know I can, Mercy. I can burn every feather off that bird of yours and then take off. I'm sick of you being at the job every day when it's not necessary. Relax. She told Piper that she didn't know how. *I know. And that scares us more than anything. You have to learn, Mercy. Or the fainting spell that you had will only get worse. You know that. Even though you're an immortal like us, you can still be hurt badly. At least until you find a mate. Please, for the love of us all, try and have some fun. At the very least, I want you to relax as much as you can.*

I'll try. She would too but was not making any promises. It was as hard for her to relax as it was most people to jump out of a plane, even with a parachute on. Mercy told her that she'd talk to her tomorrow, that she was at his home. *And I'll try my best to behave, but I'm not making any sort of promises to anyone.*

The house was old, probably older than Joel was, but it was tidy. The front porch was sagging a bit, but it had pretty greens on the front. Not flowers, she noticed when she got out, but salad greens. The fresh coat of paint on the front door was welcoming and friendly. The door opened, and a little girl in a wheelchair struggled to get through the opening.

"Here, honey, let me help you." Joel ran up the steps, skipping the first one, she noticed. It wasn't until she was ready to step up on it to join them that they both screamed at her to stop. "I'm sorry. I should have warned you. That step is off. I've tried fixing it, but I think there is something wrong with the foundation. Mercy Dante, I'd like for you to meet my daughter, Miley. Miley, this is the woman that I was telling you about."

"Hello. My dad said that you were going to be helpful to

us." Joel warned his daughter to behave. "He says that to me a lot. Like I'm going to be able to cause any trouble any other way but with my mouth."

"He's told me to behave as well. I've actually thought about ignoring him and having fun with him, but he is a stick in the mud at times." Miley laughed. It was a sound that Mercy thought that she could get used to. It was childish, of course, but it was more. Like if she could bottle it, she'd be able to quit working all together. "I can help you with your homework, if you'd like. I've done a great deal of research on it. We can even play around on the computer, and I can show you things that aren't quite true too."

"We don't have a computer, Miss Dante. But I will take the help. It's hard at times to do stuff, but Dad and I make up for it with just having fun." Mercy told her that she was sorry. "No need to be. You haven't any idea about us, and that's okay too. Come on in and I'll show you what I have to do. Dad can finish up dinner while you help me."

"I don't know." Joel seemed as if he'd rather her not help his daughter, and that pissed her off. Of course, everything did lately, but she wasn't going to change her mind. Until he spoke again. "Miley, that's something you and I work on. I'll miss that."

Reaching out to Jude, she asked her if she had any contacts that would work with her where she was. *Yes, several. Have you figured it out yet, by the way? If not, you're in New Mexico. Stay with Joel, honey, or you could be in trouble.* She knew of the recent trouble that was happening to tourists. Mercy figured that Blaze thought she could handle herself. *Why did you want to know about contacts?*

I would like for you to have someone bring a computer, as well as all the things that might need to go with it. I doubt they have Internet here, so perhaps you could get that fixed up as well.

Whatever is needed to help a child with their homework. She said that she could do that. *I'll pay for it, by the way.*

No worries there, Mercy. These people, most of them anyway, owe me a favor or two, so they'll bring it out. She heard Jude's fingers clicking across the keyboard as she spoke. *I can have cable out there in a few minutes. The hookups are there, but there isn't any service at the moment. I don't think, from what it looks like, that it ever has been.*

In less time than it took for Miley to pull out her books while her father was in the kitchen working, she not only had cable hooked up with all the stations, but also the Internet at the highest speeds. Jude told her that Joel might not care for her doing this.

Like I care. His daughter was nice to me while he was an ass. I'll take care of him if it comes to it. She might come and live with me as an orphan again. That wasn't nice, and she knew it, but she was sick of this forced vacation and being saddled with an over the top male that bossed her around.

Twenty minutes later a large truck pulled up in front of the house. The knock at the door had Joel coming from the kitchen to answer it as she was reading over the rules for the paper that Miley had coming due. It was too complicated for a child, she thought, and then looked up at Joel when he said her name.

"Mercy, I'd like to speak to you please. In private." She asked him about what. "Would you please get up off your ass and come to—?" He let out a long breath. "I'd like to talk to you about this delivery that I'm not accepting."

"You most certainly are. It's not for you anyway, it's for Miley. To help with school." She directed the men to bring in the things that Jude had set up. "It is a bit more than I thought she'd send. I only asked for a computer and whatever went with it."

"This isn't staying." She ignored him for the paperwork. "Did you hear a word I just said to you? These things aren't staying. You'll have to send them take it back."

After closing the door on the men, she turned to look at him. But she was distracted by him standing there with an apron around his waist as well as flour in his hair. He wasn't just appealing at this moment, but sexy. Mercy licked her lips, thinking of what this man could do for her that none other would.

"Stop it." She looked at him in the face. His voice was low and tight. "Stop looking at me like I'm a piece of steak."

"I'm not."

Joel growled at her. Before she could tell him to more than likely to fuck off, Miley squealed. It set off her bird to think that someone could be harming the little girl. It took her a full minute to realized that the child was excited.

"Look, Dad. Not only a computer, but a tablet too. And a printer. I've never seen this one before, even at school."

She was tearing into another box when Joel took Mercy by the hand and nearly dragged her to the bedroom. As soon as the door was closed, Mercy was pressed against the door with Joel's mouth on hers.

His hands tore at her clothing. When his nails scraped over her flesh, making small wounds, he licked them. Christ, she was as wet as she'd ever been before. Joel had her breast bared, her bra torn to pieces. The heat of his mouth on her nipples, the way that he suckled hard on them, made her have little climaxes that devastated her body all the same.

The knock at the door had her moaning. Joel pulled away from her and stared at her. Covering herself when she saw the look on his face, a look of distain, she turned away from him and moved away from the door so that he could leave her alone.

29

Mercy wasn't sure what to do now. Her body was on fire from what he'd done to her. His cock was stiff and hard too — she could see it as he left her alone in the room. But first things first, she needed to be dressed.

Being nearly naked made her feel stupid and confused. Dressing in the identical clothing that she'd had on before, Mercy decided it was time for her to stay. But the moment that she walked through the door, she could see that things were not going to be any better between them. The cable, it appeared, had been hooked up.

"I suppose this is your doing too?" She nodded and looked at Miley, who was staring at them like she was watching a good tennis match. Joel spoke through his teeth, his anger evident all over his body. "I will talk to you about this later."

"She's staying for dinner, Daddy. Right?" Joel looked like he could have easily bitten a nail in two when Miley asked him. Instead of saying anything, he walked, more like stomped, his way into the kitchen.

Mercy felt like she'd run a marathon and had come in dead last. Her body was spent and her mind a whirl of thoughts, not a one of them suitable for the child with her. As she tuned into what Miley was saying to her, Mercy realized how happy she was to have gotten the things today.

It took her until dinner was ready to get everything hooked up for Miley, and with only one contact with Jude. The printer was hooked up too — wireless, she found out — and three reams of paper to use on it. There was also a tablet, a camera, and a printer for pictures. Speakers to use on the stereo that had been brought in, as well as a big screen television. No wonder he was pissed. Jude had gone slightly overboard.

Dinner was quiet except for Miley. She talked about her project as well as the things in the living room. Not the things themselves, but the boxes and what to do with them. There were, of course, a great many of them.

"I'd not put them all out at once. And if you can cut them down and put them under your trashcan for pick up day, you won't be announcing to the world that you've gotten all this." Miley asked her why. "People will pick off houses that have gotten a payday like this one. So to keep yourself safe, just put them out one at a time, and never before trash day."

"Are you familiar with the type of person that robs houses?" Joel was baiting her, and she didn't care. The joy on Miley's face was much too wonderful for him to put her in a pissy mood. So, Mercy told him that she was, as a matter of fact. "I just bet you are."

"Dad, what is wrong with you?" Miley apologized about her dad's behavior. "He's usually so nice to people. It must be something that happened at work."

"You have no idea. Some people will just throw themselves in front of you to get what they want."

Mercy glared at Joel and pushed her plate away. The food now would catch in her throat, and she wanted to be gone.

He seemed to be in a better mood after that. She knew that it was because he thought he'd won. Perhaps he had. But she was finished with him driving her around, too. He could take the money or not; at this point, she didn't give a shit any more.

As soon as the meal was finally at an end, she picked up her plate and took it to the sink. Miley said that she was going to bed, that she'd play with her things tomorrow, and that left the two of them alone in the kitchen.

"I would like for you to take me to my hotel." He said he'd be glad to do, but the dishes needed washing up. "I don't care about your stupid dishes, I want you to take me to my hotel right now."

"I won't leave the dishes undone simply because you have a burr up your ass about how poor Joel didn't praise your name for intruding into our life when you had no right to." She said she was helping Miley, not him. "And the big screen television? The cable? I can't afford that. You will have it shut off."

"There won't be a charge for it. Someone that Jude knows has done it for you." He snarled at her, then asked if she had fucked him too. "You bastard."

The slap to his face was hard, she knew it was. But when he came at her, his face set, she backed away from him, fearful that she'd somehow gone too far. As soon as he drew back—to slap her back, she thought—Mercy felt her bird curl away from him, as if she was afraid too.

But instead of slapping her, he jerked her body to his by grabbing a handful of her hair. Her clothing was ripped from neck to hem again. This time he kissed her with a savagery that she'd never experienced before, what her body seemed to crave. Only from this man.

He picked her up by her ass. The only thing that her body wanted was to wrap around him, so she curled her legs around his hips as he took them to the bedroom again. Before they were even in the room, the door shut behind them, she was naked, his cock at her entrance.

Setting her on her feet, he held her while she tried to regain some of her equilibrium. But it was all in vain. As soon as he dropped to his knees, Joel was making a feast of her pussy.

Being quiet during sex had never been hard for her. But when he gave her pleasure, her body coming over and over, it was difficult for her to remain standing, much less keep her screams to herself. Reaching out into the room, she quieted it, made it so that no one would hear her, and let go of the blood

32

thirsty scream that had been building up inside of her.

He fucked her with his fingers, then his tongue. Mercy was weak with his ministrations. And while her body was limp from coming so many times, she wanted more, needed more from him. When he stood up, his cock wet at the tip, her body came again without his touch, she was that primed for him.

Touching him with her finger, she took the hot juices to her mouth. When the precum of him touched her tongue, she moaned loudly, needing him more than she had before. Getting down on her knees before him, she took him into her mouth and swallowed around him. His cum filled her mouth and throat almost immediately.

The need to have him inside of her made Mercy reckless. Standing up, his cum still dripping from her lips, she watched him as she cleaned herself off with her tongue. The savage growl from him nearly brought her to her knees. And when he lifted her again, slamming his cock so deep inside of her that she hurt from it, Mercy screamed.

The bed touched her back. Joel was fucking her like he meant for her to never forget him. She wouldn't. He was her first — the first human to have ever wanted her.

"Come now, Mercy. Come again for me." She did what he told her — commanded her really. No sooner had she came when she felt him come as well. His body had been hard before, muscles on top of muscles, but when he came, it was as if Joel had been created out of stone, his body harder than anything she'd ever felt.

After coming so many times that she hurt with it, Mercy felt exhaustion take her under. She knew that she should go back to her hotel, but she needed to rest. When Joel wrapped around her, held her tightly to his body, Mercy fell into a deep sleep.

33

Mercy felt the dream come over her, the same dream of her and Dante on their last day. The day that she had ended her life to begin theirs. Their conversation was as clear to her tonight as it had been every night since that day. But this one was different; this one was held in the house of Joel and his little girl.

"They need you." Mercy said that they only needed money. "Perhaps, but not all of it, and you know that you can help Miley. She needs someone to make sure that she's going to make it in this world, this world of humans."

"What is it you're trying so hard not to tell me?" Dante laughed. It was still the same as it had always been, before the king and his decree. Dante laughed like a braying jackass. It was loud and punctuated by snorts of breath. "Tell me, Dante. For this is interrupting the best sleep I've had in ages."

"You will come to love him." Mercy said that she didn't think so. "Ah, but I do. You are already nearly in love with his child. It will be only a few more pushes in the right direction for you to love them both much more than you ever did me. And that is the way it should be."

"I don't like where this is going. Tell me why you're really here, and let me rest. This is the reason for me to have done this vacation thing, to rest." She didn't mention that she'd also been told to get laid, but that wasn't really any of her queen's business. "Go away or tell me why you've come here of all places."

"Joel is a good man. Smart, and has a degree in engineering. He could help the right company, say the one that Piper has. Think how much more she would get done if she didn't have to have so many trial and errors." Mercy asked her why he didn't do that for a living. "Because, my dear, he is without means to have someone help him get Miley back and forth to her physical therapy, as well as being able to go to class. I think that Piper could work around that for him. Or she could pay him enough that he could well afford help."

"He lives here, not where we do." Dante laughed again, and then asked her if there were no houses in that area. "I don't want him that close. What will happen to...? He just can't live that close. I don't want him to."

"I see. So, you'd rather he suffered, and his child as well." It wasn't a question, but she still had no answer even if it was. "Do the right thing by him, Mercy, and good things will come your way. I can promise you this."

The dream ended, and she felt at peace. Mercy knew that she was going to help him, to make sure that he had all that he needed. And when she turned over to sleep, she reached for Joel and found him gone. Waking up, thinking that something had happened to Miley, she looked around for him, and found him staring at her from the chair across the room.

Mercy didn't have to ask if he was angry. It was written all over his face and body. He was stiff with it—not sexy like before, but like he would stab her with it if he could. Sitting up, she pulled the sheet up over her breasts, suddenly feeling very naked around him.

"Isn't it a little too late for that?" She was confused and hurt by his tone. "Did you get what you wanted, Mercy?"

"I'm sorry?" He shook his head and stood. Joel's pacing was in angry strides too. She could almost feel sorry for the floor. "I don't know what you—"

"Isn't it what all wealthy women do when they go on a vacation? They get laid? Well, you sure gave as good as you got, I'll tell you that much." Mercy didn't know what to do. Her heart, not usually so fragile, was breaking apart in her chest. "Your friend was right when she hooked you up with me, I'm thinking. Lonely broke man with a handicapped daughter who could use a good fuck too. I have to ask, did I pay for it all? I mean, you did pay up front before you fucked me. But I want to make sure you got your money's worth for all the stuff you bought for my daughter. That was slick of you too, buying for her so that I'd not get it right away. However, if it makes you feel any better, it was a nice fuck for me. Got my rocks right off."

Mercy stood up, letting him see her body. She looked down at herself, the way he might see her. The marks he'd put on her skin were there. The bruises from his hands, the bite marks from his teeth. She didn't or hadn't regretted any of it, but now she was shattered.

Without saying a word to him, she went to the window. After opening it, feeling the heat once again as it tried in vain to warm her frozen heart, she looked at him as the shift from woman to bird slowly consumed her.

When she was her falcon, Mercy hopped up to the window sill. She never took her eyes off him as she dropped out of sight. The looks, the pain of his hatred towards her, nearly had her hitting the ground without spreading her wings.

Mercy flew around for several hours, avoiding places where she might have been seen. The trees not far from where Miley lived were sparse and dry, so she stayed close to the bark where she could blend in.

Trying her best not to think of what he'd said to her, the way he'd made what they'd done feel dirty, she reached out to Piper and told her what she wanted to do.

"Is he any good? Well, of course he would be. Why would you recommend him if he wasn't? I'll call him today." Mercy warned her that he'd not take the job if she mentioned her or that they were friends. "Something happen, Mercy?"

"Yes, but I'm not going to talk about it. Perhaps never. And I have no idea if he's any good. Dante came to me in a dream and told me that he'd be perfect for you." Piper asked her if she was coming home. "Not yet. I don't think I can. Don't tell anyone that you've spoken to me. Please? I don't have it in me to answer any questions at the moment. Maybe never."

"Mercy, I'm so sorry. Is there anything I can do? Come to you?" She told her no, that she was going to be out for a while and to only contact her if necessary. "All right. And his daughter, you say that she has some troubles with her wheelchair?"

"Yes, it's very old and worn out. Out of date too, I would imagine. If you have to, Piper, tell him that he's qualified for insurance right away and that it's the best there is. Send me the bill and I'll take care of it. In fact, I insist." She said that she would, but Mercy could almost hear all the questions that were going through Piper's mind. "Remember what I said, don't mention me at any time. Dante said he'd work for you, so he'll be just what you need. And if you want him to stay, then I'd keep me out of it."

"All right. But Mercy, you have to tell me why I'm doing this and you're not." Mercy said nothing, her heart crumbling yet again over his words, his views of what had happened between then. "Okay, if you don't want to talk now, know that I'm here for you. I'll let you know what happens, all right?"

"Yes, all right. I'm going to be away for a while. I'll be back when I can."

Which, her heart was telling her, would be never. She'd done right by him and Miley. Mercy had done what Dante had told her. Taking off to the skies again, she only looked back at the house once. It was enough to tell her that she was doing the right thing, and no matter what he said, it hadn't been a vacation fling. Joel was her mate.

Chapter 3

Joel was not only impressed with the large, well-appointed building, but with the way that Miss Warrior had some of her work displayed in different parts of the lobby. The large piece, a phoenix, sat atop a perch that looked like a turret of a castle. The colors were beautiful. Joel felt like he could put out his hand and it would land on it.

"Mr. Oliver?" He stood up, nervous for this interview. The woman smiled at him. "I'm Piper Warrior. We're not very formal around here, you'll see. Let me show you around a little bit, then I'll take you to your office."

He was right behind her when what she had said occurred to him. "My office? I don't understand, I thought this was only an interview."

"No, this is a job for you to take should you want it. And I certainly hope that you do. I've looked into your work, Joel, and you're very good at what you did for your other company. May I ask why you quit?" He told her that he had a handicapped daughter. "Good for you, putting family first. As I was saying, you're very good, and I've decided that I'd be a fool not to hire you. And I'm not a fool. Silly at times, but never a fool when it comes to what I do."

"Your work, it's beautiful. The phoenix out front, it looks so lifelike." She smiled at him, her pride showing through. "If I'm to take the job, I have to tell you, I'm broke. I'm not usually so honest with a job interview, or whatever this is, but I can't afford to travel back and forth from my home. It's quite a commute."

"Yes, I can see that it would be. But that's been taken care of as well. I have a house for you and your daughter to live in. It's part of your package. As I said, I'm not a fool, and I need you to come and work for me. There is a car, big enough to put a wheelchair in should you wish to use it after work. I have also arranged to have your daughter's records transferred here. The local school is brilliant, and happy to have Miley as a student. Also, there is a cook for the house that —"

"Wait, wait. This is too fast. Not to mention, too much. I'm just a guy with a good engineering degree. How do you even know if I can work with you? I don't even know what it is you want me to do." Again, the smile. And he remembered the last time a woman smiled at him and Joel pushed it away. "I don't want to get here, move my daughter and I nearly across the United States, only to find out that I can't do whatever it is that you need."

"I think we should see your office."

Joel was getting frustrated and wanted to talk to someone. But he'd ruined that for himself by being a prick. And on top of pushing away a beautiful woman, he'd also made it so that his daughter would barely speak to him anymore. His life sucked right now.

The office was perfect. There was a huge window that he could look out over the river. A drawing board, and several large bulletin boards as well. The desk wasn't one that he'd thought to have. This one was wood, old wood too, and as smooth as — His mind skittered away from that thought. He leaned against the large credenza that sat under the window, where he could see pictures of Miley and him together. Joel looked at Piper.

"Tell me what the catch is." She leaned against the door jamb and asked him what he meant. It was then that he noticed his name was already printed on the door. "You may not believe this, but I'm not stupid. I know that there is something going on. Tell me."

"All right. But I'd like you to know, regardless of what Mercy told me about you or what to do, I'd still have hired you." He asked why Mercy was doing this. "I have no idea. I don't know where she is, what she's up to, nor do I have the ability to ask her. I guess I could, but she said to leave her alone, and we are."

"You're what she is, a bird." She nodded, then shook her head. "You're not a bird? Please, explain."

"I'm a phoenix. Just like the one out in the lobby. It's what I guess you'd call a self-portrait. When I started out, I only did smaller things — jewelry and such. But I wanted to do something more. Have fun with my heat and metals. And without you, I can't do all the things that I wish to do. I need an engineer to show me how to make — engineer — the things I want without them falling down on my head. Would you like to see her?" He shook his head. "Suit yourself. You will eventually. It's how I get the heat I need to make the pieces. For some reason I was granted the gift of fire. And I use it to make my art. If you come into my lab, you'll see me at work as well."

Joel tried to wrap his mind around all this and had to sit down. "Are there more of you? Bird shifters." She told him that they weren't shifters. "But you can shift. Correct?"

"Oh yes, and we can do it in any way that we wish. From

41

your questions, I'm assuming that you saw Mercy shift?" He nodded. "Well, she's good at it. Lots of practice, I guess, when we were working on it. Anyway, we're not shifters. We were, all six of us, birds before we were made into warriors. Larger than a semi in order to save the kingdom."

"Kingdom?" She told him about the castle and the queen. "You're...I don't mean to be rude, but I'm assuming that you're very old."

"Yes. Very. And again, Mercy is older than the rest of us. Not by much, but she was with the queen longer than us. So she was very beloved by Queen Dante. You will notice that we all took a last name that was a part of our lives before. Mercy is Dante, from our queen." She moved into the office and closed the door. "What happened between the two of you? I'm assuming that she hurt you badly."

"No, she didn't do a thing to me. It was me that hurt her. Not physically—I don't think it would have come to that. I know it wouldn't have. But I tore into her after...the next morning, and she left me. Not that I wouldn't have done the same should someone had spoken to me that way, but.... My daughter hates me for what I did. All she knows is that I was pissed off at Mercy—for no reason, I figured out later—and she left her. They clicked, you see. My daughter and Mercy." Piper said nothing. "I've been reading up on shifters. I don't actually know any, I don't think, but I have a feeling that she's something to me. Mercy, I mean."

"Yes—your mate, I would guess. And yet she did all this for you." Joel said that he didn't understand it either. "I don't think, now that I've said that, she did any of this for you, Joel. She did this for Miley."

"I see. So I have this wonderful opportunity, after I hurt a woman that should mean the world to me, because of my little girl." He looked out the window, turning his back to Piper. "I said terrible things to her. Things that any man should have been killed over. I would have done it myself had I heard another man say those things. Everything a man could ever want has fallen into my lap, and I haven't any idea what to do about it."

"Work for me, if for no other reason than to provide for Miley. I've not met her, but she must have made an impression on Mercy." Piper stood up just as he turned back to look at her. "There is a secretary for you that starts after lunch. I'm having lunch brought in so that everyone can meet you. If you decide not to work for me, let me know as soon as possible. I won't embarrass either of us by having to explain why—"

"I'm going to take the job. I'd be a bigger fool than I already think I am if I didn't." She thanked him. "No, you should be thanking Mercy. And if you see her, could you—?"

"No, I won't relay messages for you. Besides, I wasn't supposed to tell you. Mercy had a feeling that you'd run for the hills if I did." He said that a month ago, he might have. "Good. You've had time to think. All right, I know that you're at the hotel, but I can have your daughter moved to your home today. The car you are going to be using is in the parking lot if you'd rather pick her up. Here is the address. And before you ask, no, it's not near Mercy. You're on your own finding her. Your health insurance started this morning, and there is no clause for preexisting illnesses or injuries. Your house information is in there as well." She handed him a piece of paper and a thick file.

"I still have the job? After everything I told you?" Piper said that he did. "Thank you. I'll get Miley and take her there now, if that's all right."

"Yes, I'm not expecting you to work until Monday, and since it's only Wednesday, I'd take in the sights and see what the area has to offer you." She started away and came back.

"As I said, there are six of us. All birds of prey. Fuck up and we'll raise your daughter as our own. Do I make myself clear?"

"Yes, very much so." She left him there, and he stood up then sat down again. This was much more than he had ever dreamed of having. When his new secretary came in, introducing herself as Maggie Sandalwood, he was handed two cell phones. "Two?"

"Yes, Piper wanted your daughter to be able to talk to you anytime she wishes." She handed him yet another file. "Those are the things that I can do for you. I'm to tell you that I'm a wolf. Most of the people here are ex-cons getting a second chance. Anything you need, my home number is there for you to use. But not after ten unless you're in deep shit. All right?"

After telling her that he understood, he asked what time the meeting was. Maggie told him that it had been changed until tomorrow, and that they wanted to meet his daughter then too, if possible. Joel went home feeling like a man on the edge. It was almost too good to be true, and perhaps it was.

~*~

Miley was trying her best not to be too excited. They were going to have a house to live in. All she could think about was that it wasn't going to be any different than the one they had in New Mexico—a house, and not a home. When her dad had picked her up a little while ago, she could tell he was feeling the same thing—not expecting too much in the way of housing.

"This is your car?" Dad said that it was their car. "Yes, well, I don't think I'm going to be driving anytime soon. Not even later."

"I'm sorry, Miley. I didn't mean that the way it came out." She waved him off. "Piper wants to meet you. The staff does. I don't know what that'll entail, but you're to come to a meeting with me tomorrow. Is that all right with you?"

"Yes, I guess. This house, do you know anything about it? Is it in the worse part or town or something?" He shook his head while he drove carefully. The car even smelled new to her. "Did you ask them about the school I was going to go to?"

"Maggie said that there was information in the folder she gave me. Oh, before I forget." He pulled out a cell phone and handed it to her. It was the best on the market. She'd been looking at them for so long. Handing it back to him, she only said that it was nice. "That one is yours. I have one just like it. I guess it's programed with my number, as well as Maggie's. Don't call her after ten. She said she'd make me regret it unless it was a dire emergency."

"Mine? This is mine?" He said that it was a perk of the job, for her to be able to talk to him whenever she wanted. "Then I can only use it to call you. I see." It was like having cake and ice cream with this and having it taken away.

"No, Miley, it's your cell phone to use as you want. It has unlimited data, and it has a lot of apps already loaded on it. You can finally open yourself a social media account. But I want you to be careful with it." She promised that she would. "Also, we have insurance. It started today. So that means when I cut myself again, I don't have to duct tape it closed and hope it doesn't get infected."

She remembered that day. He'd been trying to cut a roast in half so that they could have it another day too. But the knife had slipped and had gouged out a long slice around his wrist. Miley had been terrified that he'd cut his wrist and was going to bleed out before help could arrive.

"Dad, why are they being so nice to us?" He told her what he'd heard from Piper. "I told you that she was nicer than you said."

"And I have since changed my mind about that too. It was all on me." He'd said that too. Two days after Mercy had left, Miley found him in his room sobbing about how he'd done Mercy wrong, said things that were mean and hurtful. And that he'd driven her away by his hatefulness. It had taken her another two days to figure out that Mercy wasn't human — she'd found a feather by the window — and that her dad had fallen in love with the woman.

Miley maybe be only thirteen, but she wasn't stupid. And she loved Mercy as well. She was someone that she could have looked up to, someone that she thought she could talk to. Yes, she told herself that they had only had a few hours together, and Miley assured herself that it wasn't the gifts but the woman. Mercy was a very nice person.

Dad whistled when the car came to a stop. Miley looked where he was looking and had to remember to shut her mouth. Goodness, this was their house? She asked her dad if he had the right address.

"Yes. I looked three times. See the numbers on the wall there? That's it. And this is the street too." He got out and came around to get her wheelchair for her. "I have to tell you, Miley, my girl, it's much easier to get this sucker in and out with all this room, isn't it?"

"I know. And you don't cuss nearly as much either." They were both laughing as they made their way to the house. "Dad, look. There's a wheelchair ramp for me. She thought of everything."

The ramp was newly made. Dad pointed out that the wood still had the lumber marks on it. And as he pushed her up the nice wide ramp, he pointed at the rockers on the front porch, the flowers in the window boxes. This was, she thought, just too good to be theirs.

The house was one level. And as soon as they entered the

double doors, Miley looked at her dad. The place was beautiful. There was furniture in this room that she had dreamed of all her life. And there was a fireplace, and a big picture window that looked out over the trees behind the house. Miley could just imagine the Christmas tree there in a few months, with actual presents under it this year.

Miley never complained about the lack of money to her dad. He was doing the best he could. He never missed work, even when he was very sick, but he'd take the day off if she had just the sniffles. Dad was the best possible person that a child like her could have had.

She didn't remember her mom, nor the accident that had taken her life. Miley had been told last year how she'd ended up with her dad. And she was so happy every day that he'd been willing to take her. The accident had left her so that no one at the adoption agency would be able to give her a loving home. Only one that, she knew, could see her raped or killed because of how she had to have extra care.

They moved through the house like they were afraid to touch anything. When they entered the big warm kitchen a woman was there, kneading bread, and she had on a big smile. Miley liked her immediately.

"My name is Dutch. Last name...? I don't rightly remember if I had one or not. But you can just call me Dutch." Dad told her their names. "The miss, she told me that you'd be coming around today, and that I was to tell you if you don't like the way the house is filled, you just tell Miss Piper and she'll be the one to fix you up. I can serve you dinner anytime you want. Just you let me know any of your likes and dislikes."

"What time will dinner be ready?" She grinned at her, and Miley grinned back. "I'm betting that you knew Mercy when she was with the queen."

"I did. You know about that, do you?" Miley nodded.

47

"Well, I did know her way back in the beginning. She wasn't no human back then, though. Just a giant bird with them others. You'll meet them soon enough, I'm thinking. But Miss Mercy, she was sure the favorite of the queen. And oh, what a wonderful queen she was. Kept us safe in the keep when all the other kings and queens were killed, and their people too. Then that nasty king of the land, he decided that Lady Dante would be his wife. Do you know what she did? Why, that queen, she came out to see us and told us that she'd be taking care of us all. That we only had to do what she asked, and no one would kill them off for their own people. And she did it too. Now. What can I make so that you'll be able to not starve between now and dinner time?"

While she ate cheese and an apple, Dutch told them about the queen and how she'd come to move them. If she hadn't believed in magic before, she did today. And when she went to her room, finally, Miley sat in the middle of the large room after looking all around it and cried.

"What's the matter, honey?" Dad helped her to sit on the bed, but it would have been easy for her to do it herself. "Do you not like it? Or this house?"

"Dad, she made it so that my room is perfect. Look. I have a view to outside, and I can slide out onto the deck back there. I have a big bed that is low enough that I can get in and out of it all by myself. The bathroom has a specialized tub so that I can get in and not splash water everywhere. There's everything in there just for me and my wheelchair. And look at that over by the closet."

The wheelchair was what had got her crying. It was padded, though she wouldn't be able to feel it, and the wheels that she used were small and easier for her to turn. All she wanted to do was to hop on it and take a ride around the room. But she needed a minute.

"It's motorized as well, Miley." He showed her where the little arm was that she could us. "The instructions say that it's for going uphill easier, as well as when you need a break. Then it says, it's all right for you to need a break once in a while."

That set her off crying again. Mercy had done so much for them and never, not once, said a thing about it. Looking at her dad through her tears, she wondered briefly if she should tell him that she spoke to Mercy nearly every day. But she'd made a promise, one that she knew she had to keep for a bit longer.

Dad's room was bigger, of course, and so nice. The bed was giant, and she wondered if Mercy had done that for them, then dismissed that thought. Mercy said she wasn't going to see her dad anymore, that she was just too busy. Miley hurt for the two of them. But at least she knew that Mercy was thinking of them too, and that might be good.

There were other things that she could tell her dad, things that she'd been sworn to secrecy about unless he figured them out. Then she could tell him where the magic had come from. But before then, she was just to use what she'd been given, and try very hard not to freak her dad out. Mercy said that in time, he'd have it all, but for now, he could figure it out a little at a time. She hoped her dad was curious enough to figure it out soon. She was excited for him to get freaked out and call to Mercy. If he would.

~*~

Mercy wasn't going to tell the others that she'd been in and out of the plant for the last week or so. She supposed that Blaze would have figured it out by now. She'd been leaving her notes on things since she'd been back, and Blaze was making them work. The new policy was getting rave reviews.

One month off in the summer months for every employee

that had perfect attendance. With pay. And, if they got through a year without injury that was their own fault, then they got a bonus at Christmas time. But the injury wouldn't count against them if it was deemed the company's fault. Mercy had told Blaze to try to be extra lenient about laying fault at the employee's door.

Production was at an all-time high, and orders were coming in heavily. It was still nine weeks until Christmas, but stores would need product now for it. So long as they ordered by the eighteenth of December, Mercy and Blaze would try to have their orders to them on time. It made for a good relationship with them. She thought about the note from Blaze.

You really should go and see him. He and Miley are loving the house, and you should have been at the meeting when we welcomed Joel to the family. That was rude of you.

Blaze had been the one that would always tell her when she was wrong. Well, they all would be, but Blaze was less nice about it than the other four. Today proved that not only was Blaze getting pissed off at her, but she'd also threatened to tell Joel and Miley where she lived.

Leaving her a note to change things, Mercy decided to ignore her threat. She might tell them, but Mercy could hide better than anyone could. She'd been at it a good deal longer, and she had more magic than the others too.

Mercy knew that she'd have to go and see Joel soon enough. There were things going on that he would need to be made aware of. For one thing, she figured out that she could make it so that Miley could walk. It wasn't something that she'd been looking for but reading up on the magic that she'd been left by the queen, it stated that if someone, in this case Miley, were close to her heart, then she could do a great many things to that person that would enhance their life.

50

She figured that walking was something that would enhance anyone's life.

Then there was the child. She had gotten knocked up, it seemed, and wasn't really sure how she felt about that. Nor, for that matter, how he'd feel about it. According to the book that she'd read again, it would appear that Joel was what she was—a falcon. Just because of the magic of finding her mate.

"Mother fuck. He's going to be pissed about it all, I just know it."

It had been five weeks since she'd been with Joel, less since she and Miley had talked. The girl was smart, much smarter than people gave her credit for.

Picking up the phone for the hundredth time in the last two hours, she placed the call to his cell phone. Maybe, she thought, he'd not answer it. She'd made sure that her number would be blocked, and maybe he was—

"Yes, hello?" Fuck, he would be the type to answer. "Hello? This is Joel Oliver. Has something happened to my daughter?"

"It's Mercy." She waited while he didn't speak, waiting for him to hang up the phone, or worse yet, tell her to fuck off. "I would like to set up a time to speak to you about some things."

"Anytime. I'm on my lunch hour now if you'd like to come here. I'm so glad you called, Mercy. I have so much to tell you too." He laughed a little. "The house. I can't thank you enough for it. And everything else."

"How did you...? Blaze. Or Piper told you." He said that it was a guess, but she knew that they'd spoken to him. "Can you come here now? Or after work? I get off at four and should be home about four thirty. Miley will be thrilled to see you."

Mercy wanted to cancel this. Not to see him. She also wanted to ask him if he'd be glad to see her as well. When he asked again when she was coming to see him, she told him that it would be later, after dinner.

"I can't wait to see you, Mercy. It's been a long time, and I have so much.... I'm so very sorry for the way I treated you that morning. You have no idea how badly I feel for what I did to you." She cried, her eyes burning with the tears. "I love you, Mercy. I don't know how it happened, and frankly, I don't care. But I do love you. I think I have from the moment that I saw you."

"You hurt me." Joel said that he knew he had. And it hurt him that he'd done that to her. "I don't know what I feel about you. I hurt with every breath I take that you said those things to me."

"If I could do it all over, I'd never say that to you. But it's too late to try and not say that stuff. I truly regret it. I'm so sorry, Mercy." She heard someone talking to him. "I have to go. You'll be there tonight, won't you? I'd like to ask you to promise me, but I don't deserve that. Just, please, I'm begging you to come tonight."

She placed the receiver in the cradle. Mercy regretted calling him, and at the same time was glad that she had. They really did have to talk, if for no other reason than to make him aware of a few things. Not even counting the baby.

Mercy put her hand over her flat belly. A child grew there, and she had no idea if it would be magical, like she was, or something else. Just yesterday she'd gone to see the old doctor, the one that had been at the castle when they had been. He'd been less than helpful.

The man was a loon, she decided, and wondered if he saw many patients anymore. She was going to put the word out that everyone should avoid him from now on. His medical practices were of the old ways. He'd actually suggested to her that he find some leeches to bleed out the poison in her body. Walking away from him was much better than she had wanted to do. The old buzzard was lucky to be alive.

"Now I have to figure out how to tell Joel he's going to be a father again."

Mercy walked around her office. The apartment she was living in was much too small for her, but as she rarely stayed here, it had suited her just fine. Now, with a baby coming, she realized that she didn't have the room for much of anything. It was time to look at bigger houses.

The one that Joel and Miley lived in wasn't suitable either. Yes, it was bigger than her apartment, but it only had two bedrooms and a smallish one that Joel was using for an office. The only thing that it had going for it was the fact that it had a large kitchen. Mercy didn't cook, but she did love to eat.

Standing in front of the mirror, she tried out several different outfits and discarded them all. She wanted to wear something that said she didn't give a fuck what he wanted, but also showed that she was all woman. Nothing that she could think of, it seemed, did both of those at the same time.

Sitting down at her computer, she started looking for homes. It would be big, she decided. And if he were to want to raise their child part of the time, without her, she wanted something that was close to the others. The six birds, she thought, could have a lot of fun with an infant.

There were three houses that she liked. One of them had nine bedrooms, the other eleven. But the one that she liked the most of all was the larger of the three, which sat on nearly four hundred acres of trees. It had been an arbor at one time, and now that no one took care of the trees, they were in abundance.

When it got closer to the time for her to leave, she dressed herself in a pair of jeans and a T-shirt. It was casual as well as comfy. It seemed that lately she didn't want to wear heels and dresses. The more comfortable she was, the better she liked it, even going so far as to go barefoot. Mercy had forgotten the feel of carpet and grass under her toes.

Deciding to fly rather than drive, she sat outside his home for ten minutes before Miley opened her bedroom door out into the yard. She looked beautiful in her jeans and boots. Her sweater was one that she'd shown her herself. Mercy flew down to meet the young girl.

"You're here." Mercy shifted, her body taking on the clothing that she'd decided to wear. "Dad isn't home, so we can talk."

Mercy sat on the decking and watched the yard as she told her that she was coming for dinner. That her father had invited her. Neither of them said anything for some time, and it was Miley that broke the silence.

"Are you going to tell him about the magic?" Mercy told her that was one of the things they were going to talk about. "Are you going to tell him, too, that you've been here with me?"

"Yes, I don't like that we were sneaking around. He should know, don't you think? I was afraid that if I told him before, he might forbid me to come around." Miley told her that he'd never do that. "He might yet, Miley. We didn't exactly part on good terms."

"He told me. Dad was devasted when he figured out what an ass he'd been." Mercy laughed with Miley. "I think every day, he regrets it more and more."

"We'll see. I've been meaning to ask you. How do you like your new school? I heard that it's a very good one." Miley told her that they were great, and that she wasn't as bored as she used to be. "That's good. A friend of mine runs it, and she was glad to take you in after she got all your paperwork. I'm assuming that your dad was all right with you going to a progressive school like that one instead of a traditional one?"

"Yes, he knew that I was struggling at the other school. But no one told him that it wasn't that I was behind, but that I was much too advanced to be sitting with children that weren't. The teacher, Miss Roebuck, told me that I should have been taking advanced classes all along. I might have even been out of high school by now."

The door to the house opened and neither of them moved when Joel called out for Miley. When he came to her door to the outside, Mercy felt her belly tense up. When he came out onto the deck and sat with the two of them, no one said a word until he did.

"I love the view from the back of the house. Whoever built it, they did a great thing by turning the bedrooms so that the person staying in the rooms would be able to see this first thing." Mercy didn't say anything, and Joel looked at her. "You did this, didn't you? This was something you built. Isn't it?"

"Yes, I was everything at one time or another. When you're around as long as we've been, it's easy to get bored. The tin toys that we make, they were pieces that I picked up over the centuries. And when the man who had them sort of fell into a bad place, he sold me the patent on them. I still pay his estate royalties every year, but we've made a good amount of money on them." Joel asked if she was bored with it yet. "Yes, I don't want to make toys anymore. Blaze is going to take over until we sell it off or close it down, but I'm finished with it. I'm going to have your baby, Joel."

Chapter 4

Joel didn't know what to say. He was trying to gauge her feelings on having his child. Miley was happy, screaming about having a sibling and excited to have someone to play with. Joel just kept watching Mercy.

"You're not saying anything." He asked her how she felt about it. "If you're asking me to get rid of it, then I'm going to tell you right now that I'm not."

"No, I'd never do anything like that. Never. And I would like to help you raise the baby. I have about ten thousand questions going through my head at the moment, none of them—"

"Dinner is ready, sir." Dutch smiled at her. "You'll be joining us, I assume. I have you a plate of worms and such all ready to eat, my lady."

After Dutch left, Miley looked at her, shocked.

"You're not eating worms, are you?" Miley shivered as she continued. "I don't care that you eat them, but please, eat them some other time. I don't think I could handle that."

"She's joking." Mercy looked at him again. "I only eat that sort of thing when I'm a bird. Which lately, is a lot. May

57

I still join you two?"

"Of course." She followed him to the dining room. He'd made touches throughout the house—mostly Miley would find something online and he'd buy it. It was certainly nice being able to afford things, even if they weren't something that they needed. "I don't know what we're having. I called Dutch this afternoon after talking to you to tell her that you were joining us. She acted as if she knew already."

"She did, I would imagine. I told you that she was magical, or at least Piper did." He said that he had been told. "Things have been well here? You have everything that you need?"

"Yes, I mean, we've had fun buying little things. I have a lot of pictures of Miley and some of both of us that I've gotten frames for. But I've been enjoying just being at home after working all day too. Will the baby be human?"

"No, I'm not, snd as of the moment that we touched, neither are you." Joel dropped his fork and looked at Miley when she laughed. Mercy picked up the roll that had been knocked off his plate and handed it to him. "I had to do some research on things. I was given a book on the magic when we were turned into what we are. Here, you need to drink something or breathe. You're making me nervous."

Joel drank down the entire glass of water and looked at Mercy again. "What sort of magic do I have?" She asked him if he was comfortable in his suit. "No, not really. I come home and change, but I wanted to— What the hell was that?"

"You can now just change into whatever you think about. And you should know that Miley can do that as well." They both looked at his daughter when she giggled. A dizzyingly amount of clothing changed on her body in a matter of moments. "I have had it since I was made. You, again, since we touched."

"Why a touch? What I mean is, why did just a touch

do this? I would imagine that you've touched a great many people in your time." She nodded, and said it was because they were mates. "I see. Not really, but for now, I have an answer I can work with."

"So, I can do this all the time? Change my clothing? Into anything I want?" Mercy told her that was right. Even a gown if she wanted. "Great. No more going shopping for clothing. I hate that. The rooms are much too small for me, and my wheelchair gets stuck all the time."

"I can heal you." Joel dropped his fork again. "You keep that up and I'm going to put a bib on you. You're making a mess."

"You can't say something like that and expect me not to react. What? How can you heal her? With a touch?" Mercy shook her head. Before he could ask any more questions, Miley spoke.

"I don't care what you have to do to me, so long as I can walk. I've never done that, you know that? Never taken a step in the grass. For that matter, I've never felt the grass beneath my feet. I don't know what it's like to pee in a toilet. That might seem stupid to you, but to me, it would mean the world." Miley started crying. "Dad, you have to allow her to do this for me. I want this so badly. I would have been all right with never being able to walk, but I have an opportunity to take steps that I never was able to do before."

"Miley, honey, I want you to be able to walk as well. But we have to figure it out. I'm sure that Mercy has thought of everything." He looked at her and she nodded. "See? Didn't I tell you she was the best? So, what do we have to do?"

"It's not just healing her that we have to worry about. Or be concerned about." Miley started to speak when Mercy cut her off to continue. "You've been in a wheelchair all your life, right? You haven't any idea how to walk, balance or, as you

59

said, go to the bathroom. This is going to take work. On all our parts. You have to take time to get the basics of being on your feet, doing things that require you to stand. Balance is just one of them, as I mentioned, but you will need to learn to bend at the waist, with your knees. I'm sorry to say it this way, but you're going to have to be treated as an infant. Simply because you never learned these things as one."

"Okay, I can understand that. But I'd like to get started as soon as possible. And, if we can, I'd like to keep this between us." Miley asked him if he thought it was going to fail. "No, never that. But I think that it will be a wonderful surprise when you'll be able to step out of that thing and walk, don't you?"

"Yes, yes I do. I'm so excited." Miley looked at him. He could tell that she was trying her very best to not demand that they do it now. "What do we do first?"

"You need to shift." Joel didn't even ask. He figured that if Mercy said it that way, then it was possible that Miley could shift. "You can as well, Joel. Again, since we touched. Miley can because she's in my heart. As my child."

He didn't know what to say. He wasn't even sure that he could speak around the lump in his throat. She loved his daughter—loved her like her own child. And when Miley rolled around the table to hug her, he got up to join them. Kissing them both on the head, he told them that he loved them too. With all his heart.

They were silent for a few moments, then Miley said something about breathing, a minor thing, that he laughed about when there was so much love around the room. Just as he was sitting down to eat, Mercy dropped another bombshell on them.

"You're both immortal too."

For as long as he lived, which apparently was going to

be a very long time, he didn't think he'd ever drop his fork at a meal like he had this one. Clearing his throat as the other two ate, he decided that he needed time. Or at least some guidelines about telling him things. But they were laughing, at him, and Joel found that he didn't care. He'd drop his fork the rest of his days if it made them this happy.

The process to help Miley wasn't as bad as he thought. Yes, she had to shift, which worried him more than he could admit out loud, but Miley was excited. Mercy was careful with her to the point where he could see Miley wanted to bash her head in.

"All right. So, I just think of a falcon and then wait for her to contact me." Mercy said that was right. "To be honest, I don't think I've ever seen one, except in books. Can you — I don't want to cause you any trouble, but can you make one for me?"

"It's no trouble, but my bird sometimes has a mind of her own. She may sit on your lap." Miley made a joke about not being able to feel it. "I just don't want her to get into the habit of doing it. She has great talons, as well as she is a little nippy. Don't let her if she wants to hurt you. All right?"

"Yes, but one thing first, I know that you're Dad's mate and all. And I've never called anyone this before, but can I call you Mom?"

Mercy's shift from human to falcon was swift.

"Did I make her mad?" Joel said that the bird, he reminded her, had a mind of her own. "She did say that. I hope that I didn't make her mad."

The falcon was beautiful this close up. The brown feathers on her back were soft looking, and her legs were snowy white. When the pretty but deadly bird hopped up on Miley's wheelchair, she looked as if she were showing off. But the beak was what scared him more than her talons, which were long and sharp.

"May I touch you?" The bird nodded. He supposed that the bird had a name and started thinking of her as Mercy. "You're very soft, aren't you? And you have more than just brown and white on your feathers. Some of them are black, others are orange and blue. I guess that's so you can blend in."

When Mercy grew to her large bird and spread out her wings, Joel was shocked—he'd never realized before how wide they'd be. Nearly sixty feet, he'd bet, and when she turned to look at him, he had a feeling that the bird was sizing him up.

She wants to taste you. All sorts of thoughts went through his mind. *Not like that, you moron. She'd clip you until you were nothing but a nub. She means to taste your skin. And when she does, don't touch her. It'll hurt, but she'll transfer more magic to you.*

"I'm not sure I want more magic." Mercy became her small bird again and moved to stand on the corner of the coffee table, where he was sitting. "This nip, where would she like to do it? I'm assuming it won't matter."

No. Just put out your hand. As I said, it will hurt, but you're going to be marked. To be honest, Joel, I'm not sure what that means, but she wants to mark you.

His hand was trembling, but at this point, he thought that it was all right. After today, he would have been surprised if he hadn't been trembling a little. When she spread her wings again, he watched as she flapped them quickly but didn't lift off the table. That was when she bit him. The distraction helped some, but it was very painful.

He felt it roll over him in waves. The magic, he assumed, seemed to fill parts of him that he'd not realized would matter. Even his earlobes tingled. Then the burning of his shoulder and back nearly took him to the floor.

Ripping off his shirt, he could see the tat as it made its way down his arm. He'd have a sleeve, his mind said to him, as if it were a different person. And when the warmth of blood rolled down over his arm to his wrist, he saw it then — the falcons in a neat circle around his wrist. He had a sigil to mark him as a falcon.

The bird then sat with Miley. Joel was too focused on his pain right now to realize that she was sitting on Miley's lap. Before he could tell her to be careful, to remember what Mercy had told her, the falcon bit her too, in the same place, and Miley screamed.

~*~

Mercy knew what Miley was feeling but waited for her to figure out what it was. Mercy sat on the floor in front of her, watching her face as the pain of the mark subsided. She knew just when she realized what it was that was hurting.

"I can feel it." Mercy nodded and smiled. But it took Joel a little longer to understand. "Dad, I can feel it. The cuts, I can feel them."

"Did you know that she was going to mark her too?" Mercy said she hadn't, but it was a good thing. "How do you figure that? She has a tattoo that is— What can you feel, Miley?"

Miley laughed with her. When she told her dad that she could feel the cuts on her legs, Mercy moved back so that she could be with her dad. Mercy watched the younger girl carefully. She didn't want her doing too much at first.

"She bit her so that she could be healed with her magic." Joel asked if that was all it took. "Yes and no. I guess she figured that if she were to shift, which you both could do before, she would be too weak to try and work on walking. But, I would suggest that you take it easy. If you rush this, you're going to get hurt. I don't mean you might get hurt—you will be hurt. Falling at this stage of your life would hurt badly."

Mercy was so calm. He was a mess, and there she sat, looking at his...no, their daughter, like this was something that happened every day. Miley looked at him. Her eyes were still wet, and the blood was pooled on her hand, like it had his.

"Dad, will you carry me outside? I want to just have the grass on my toes. I know that I can't walk, but this is something that I've wanted forever. Please?" He couldn't have turned her down if she'd asked him to bring the moon in the house so she could touch it. "I'll be really careful. Just set me in the grass and I'll be content for the day."

Picking her up, he realized how much bigger she was getting. Thirteen. His little girl was thirteen-years-old. Setting her on the grass was the simplest thing he could have done for her, but she looked at him as if she'd gotten everything that she'd ever wanted. Mercy sat on one of the deck chairs and he joined her.

"She can hide her marks the same as you can. Just think of them covered and they'll be gone from view. I have them too, but since I've never been one to show off what I am, they've been hidden for a long time." He could see them then, the marks that made her what she was. The one at her wrist was wider than his, a great deal wider in that it reached almost all the way to her elbow. "I have this for all the wars I've fought in. You have yours for the same reason."

"I've never been at war. I don't understand why I'd have even this one." She just looked at him. "Mercy, I love you."

"And I love you as well. but that doesn't get you off the hook so easily. You hurt me. Devasted me, in fact." He told her that he knew that. "Your war is fighting to keep your daughter from harm. By working so hard to keep her fed and safe. That is your war. And you will get one every time you do something like that for others. They'll be thinner, yes, but you'll have them."

Miley played in the grass for an hour. At one point she rolled to her belly and was able to wiggle her toes. Joel wasn't sure that she realized she'd done it, and when she sat up, leaning back on her arms, she did it again.

"I've never done that before." Miley laughed. It rang through the yard and became attached to his heart. He ached with his love for this child—and for the one that Mercy was carrying.

When Miley was tired, he took her to the couch and let her rest. She was asleep in no time, and Mercy covered her up with the coverlet that they'd just gotten last week. He asked Mercy if he could talk to her, and they made their way to his new office.

He'd really meant to talk to her. To ask her what he should know, how long would she be pregnant. But the thought of touching her, kissing her, made his cock hurt, his body tingle with anticipation. As soon as he pulled her body to his, she came to him as if she'd needed him as well.

Their clothing was gone. He loved this new magic for that. When he pressed her against the door, thinking that he'd have a chance to look at her wholly, he was backed up by Mercy until the top of the desk touched the back of his knees.

"I'll make the room so no one outside of it can hear you." He nodded, not sure what she had in mind until she got down on her knees. "I've wanted to do this so much. It's all I can think about."

Before he could say a word, even if one had formed in his mind, she took him deeply into her mouth. And like before when she'd done it, he cried out with the tightness of her throat, the way her tongue seemed to roll around him.

Joel pushed forward, thinking just to fuck her when she swallowed.

"Holy fuck a duck."

She bobbed over his cock, his body responding to the tightness of it all. Fucking her this way, having her between his legs, Joel moved her hair so that he could see her.

His cock was wet with her juices as it went in and out of her mouth. Joel felt her saliva as it rolled down over his balls. When Mercy touched him there, using her juices to roll his balls in her palm, he fucked her mouth harder.

It was not enough and too much at the same time. And when she gave his balls a tight but gentle squeeze, he cried out with his release even as he fucked her mouth over and over. But when Mercy leaned back from him, he could see her need—her skin was dewy with it.

Joel fisted his cock, using her spittle to make the slide faster and better. Mercy opened her mouth. He knew what she wanted, and he needed to come all over her so that she could taste him again.

Holding his balls—they ached with how full they were—he told her to touch herself, to make her pretty pussy beg for him. And when her fingers slid into her nether lips, she used the other hand to squeeze and tease her nipples. Christ, Joel came so hard that his back ached from it, his body bent back to make sure she got it all. Coming that hard had never happened to him before.

When she stood up, he was weak with his releases. Joel knew that she needed to come too, but he wasn't sure he could help her. That was until she leaned over his desk, her beautiful ass pointed at him, seemingly begging for him to take her this way.

Grabbing her by the buttocks, he held on as he slammed forward into her pussy. She cried out, her body tightened around him. And as he fucked her, pounded her as hard as he could, miraculously, his balls filled again and suddenly, just like that, he felt his bird or something move over him until Joel had the most urgent need to bite her shoulder.

"Do it." He leaned to her, his mouth shifting under his lips. When Mercy commanded again for him to do it, Joel sank his teeth hard into her shoulder. "Yes."

The bones beneath his mouth seemed to crack and break. He could hear it, actually, the way her bones gave under his powerful bite. And when she screamed again, he knew it wasn't from the pain of the bite, but a climax that took him over the edge with her.

Joel tried to stand upright but his body just wasn't ready yet. And when Mercy giggled, he asked her, from his position at her back, what the hell she thought was so funny. He had to laugh too when her giggling turned to laughter.

"Us. I wasn't going to do this. Not have sex with you right away. But the moment that door closed, it was like a switch had been turned on and I was wet with need." He cursed low and fluently. "Yes, well, that's about the way I feel too."

Standing, staggering only a little he was glad to see, Joel turned Mercy around and held her. He was glad to see that she wasn't in any better shape than he was. Still, he had a lot to talk to her about. Then he realized what he really wanted to say to her.

"Marry me, Mercy. I'd get down on my knees and do this, but I know that I'd never get back up. But I would like for you to become my wife. Have more children with me in addition to this one." She kissed him lightly on the mouth and nodded. "Please, say it. I want you to say you will marry me while we're both buck naked and sated."

"Yes, I will marry you while we're both buck naked and sated." It took him a moment to realize that she'd made

67

a joke. Laughing, she was dressed and moving toward the door while he was still hanging on to the desk for dear life. "You'd better hurry and recover. We're about to have some company."

Joel didn't want to have company. He wanted to go upstairs and take a long nap. For about a month. Then he wanted to rest up so that he could make it to the shower. Standing upright, he felt better, but his knees still felt like they were made of rubber. But the longer he stood there, the better he began to feel.

The company, as she called it, was his brother. Saul hadn't been around for fifteen or so years. Joel and he had never been friends, and the only reason that they had gotten together recently was when their father had been killed. Then few months later, their mom. As soon as he introduced him to Mercy, as his wife, he asked him what he wanted.

"Why is that the first thing out of your mouth every time you see me? You'd think that I was some sort of bum or something." Saul looked at Mercy, and she didn't take Saul's hand when he offered it to her. "I guess my brother has told you all about me. Well, not all of it is true. And some of that might even be a lie."

"No, I had no idea that you existed until just this moment. And you're not staying, so don't get yourself too comfortable." Saul looked at him, shocked. "What is it you want, Saul?"

"Wow, who shit in your oatmeal? Can't a man come and see his brother and his new family once without everyone being shitty to him?" Joel didn't say anything, and Mercy left them to see to Miley. "You sure made out for yourself, Joel. Nice house. A beautiful wife. No wonder you moved up from New Mexico. That's where I was looking for you. You didn't mention to anyone that you were moving out."

"Perhaps there was a reason for it. Again, what is it you

want, Saul? I don't have time for your schemes. I'm not going to give you money, nor am I going to go on any trip with you. The last time we did that, I was seventeen and you left me in another country without any money or my passport. Mom and Dad had to work hard at getting me home." Saul just waved his hand at him. "You have someplace to stay?"

"Well, I thought that I'd stay here for a few weeks. Just until I get up on my feet. You'll let me do that, won't you, little brother?" Joel told him no. Then he looked over his shoulder and he knew that Saul saw Miley. "Well well, who is this pretty little thing? I didn't think you'd marry anyone with a kid, Joel. I guess you get good benefits for taking on someone else's—"

"She's my daughter. Mercy and I are going to have a second child soon, too." Joel could see his brother's mind working. Would it be handicapped too? How did she get hurt? "Whatever you wanted, you're not getting it. So, I would suggest that you get out before you say something stupid and I'll have to break your neck."

"Aw, come on, Joel. This isn't like you." Saul laughed. "Oh, I see. You're acting up for the ladies. Well, that's fine. Just spot me come cash and I'll find a nice hotel. Just don't be too stingy with it, little bro. I have to eat too, and I'm low on gas."

Mercy went to the door and held it open. Joel went to stand beside her and was worried when Saul made his way to Miley and put out his hand, Miley slapped it away and smiled at him.

"I'd take heed on what my parents say, Mr. Oliver. Get out of our home, and don't come back." Saul told her she shouldn't talk to her elders that way. "Yes, well, I give as good as I get. Mom and Dad told you to leave, and I'd do it."

Saul went to the door and stopped to stare at the two of

them. Then he looked at him. Joel could see his anger. Saul had always had a short fuse that wouldn't burn out for a long time. When he lunged at him Joel stood his ground, and Mercy slammed the door in Saul's face when he turned to speak again.

Chapter 5

Mercy looked over the computer printout that Jude had given her. Saul Oliver was an evil man, and the only reason that he was out walking around instead of in prison was that he was lucky. But Mercy decided that his luck was about to run out.

"I think he killed our parents." Mercy looked at Joel when he spoke to her from the chair. "I never thought about it until later, after we buried Mom, that he might have had something to do with their deaths."

"How so? Not that I don't believe you, but how do you think he might have killed them?" Mercy thought that he might have too. Saul had been into a lot of things, and none of them were on the right side of the law. "So you know, for the last year Saul has been in prison. Armed robbery. He's only been out about a month, likely looking for you."

"I had nothing for him to steal before, but I have a feeling that he'll be back here, and not necessarily when we're home. I think he murdered Dad with his axe. There isn't any way that he could have fallen on it and split his head open the way that he they said he had. And Mom was so depressed after

71

Dad died that I think he played on that and helped her along with it. She didn't kill herself—I know that she didn't, but proving it was nearly impossible without the funds to hire someone to look into it." Mercy asked him if he really thought that Saul would get into the house. "He always has a way. Then he'll blame it on me, like I'd left glass in the window for him to bust out to gain entrance."

"I see. Well, I'd not worry so much about him trying to get in as much as where to bury his body if he comes here again." She was serious, but she didn't think that Joel thought she was. "By the way, I've set up a time, three days a week, for Miley to have physical therapy at the hospital. She will also be safe from the time she leaves here until she returns. I don't think that Saul will stoop to taking her, but I don't want to take the chance of him trying."

"He will if he thinks it will get him a few bucks. You said something about a house that you wanted me to look at. I don't have to be at work until tomorrow. I was hoping that I could talk you into have a nice dinner out with Miley and myself. I know we're doing this sort of backwards, but I only just realized this morning when I got up that we've never had a date."

Miley was out with Blaze this afternoon. Blaze was trying to open up a larger client base to sell to and wanted Miley's opinion on some of the pieces that she was working on. Mostly it was things to give to Grandma and Mom if a kid had a few bucks, but it was something that she'd been playing around with for some time.

"Why was he in prison?" Mercy looked at Joel, slightly confused for a moment. "Saul. Why was he in prison? I'm sure you know."

"I do. He and two other men tried to stick up a library. I kid you not, Joel, a library. Who in their right mind tries to rob a place that only lends out books? Anyway, he and one of them came out only to find that they'd parked in two spaces, and some of the patrons were pissy about it and blocked them in." Joel asked about the other man. "Oh, he was checking out a book. For Christ's sake, if I didn't know he was stupid before, this sure does show it."

They were both laughing when Jude joined them. They'd been in the office when the front door had been knocked on, and Jude just came in, sat down, and didn't say a word. Mercy and Joel talked quietly around her until she got around to speaking.

"This guy, your brother. What do you really know about him?" Joel told her nothing, other than what she'd found on him. "I dug a little deeper. I found some things that he might well have been involved in, but no one could attach his name to the crimes. Things like robbery, kidnapping, and murder. The murder one isn't recent. But the kidnapping was just a few months ago, just after he got out of prison. I mean, like the same week he got out. I'd like to not have to kill this guy. Sorry, Joel, I know he's your brother and all, but he has got to go."

"What did he do to you?" Jude's face turned bright red. "Did he make a pass at you, Jude? If he did, then you have my permission to murder him."

"No, it wasn't that. But somehow he figured out that I'm related to you. And so you know, most of the town believes that we're all sisters. I didn't tell them any different. We are anyway, from our single mindedness to stick together." Mercy thanked her. "No problem. Anyway, he figured out somehow that you're married to my sister. So, he comes to the office, telling anyone that will listen that he's going to be taking over running the place for us. You have no idea how much trouble I had to deal with before security took him out. I wish now

I'd had him buried in the back of the plant with his head just above the dirt. Do they do that anymore?"

"Did they ever?" Both Jude and Mercy nodded at Joel. "Just keep telling me not to piss any of you off again. I think I got out on the good end of the stick when I messed up with Mercy."

"If you'd like to think that, go ahead." Again, she thought Joel was assuming that Jude was kidding when they'd all been ready to kill him. Jude continued as she leaned back in her chair. "He had been asking security for a badge, one that would get him to the upper offices. Also, he is waving around money, just a handful of ones with a fifty on top, that he'll pay if someone will give them their swipe in badge. I'd hate to think what sort of things he could do to the place if he got in."

"We'll have to have the cameras watching all the doors, inside and out, and make it known that if anyone sells or even gives him their badge, they'll be terminated without regard of their years here. And if their badge is stolen, to report it immediately." Joel looked at Mercy, his face flushed with embarrassment from his comment. "I'm sorry. I should just keep my mouth shut from now on."

"Why?" He looked at Jude and told her that it wasn't his business. "Yes, it is, Joel. Everything that we have, you are now a part of. More so with what Mercy owned on her own before you and Miley came along. We were going to ask you if we could adopt her as our niece, since she calls us her aunts when she needs us. You are just as much family as we are."

"He's a falcon. So is Miley." Mercy watched the expression on Jude's face turn from concern, to making sure that Joel knew he was family, to excitement. "And we're having a baby."

"Holy shit balls. That's wonderful news. Have you told anyone else of all this?" Mercy said they'd not, but she had more. "I don't know if I can take much more. This is wonderful enough."

"I healed Miley. She can't walk yet — she has to learn how, and since she's never taken a step, she'll have to start from scratch. She's going to need all of us to keep her from trying too much at once." Jude said she would too. "Yes. I don't doubt right now she's scheming up ways to walk around the block while we're not watching."

"Yes, well, I won't let her. Remember when we had to learn to walk? That was an experience that I'll not soon forget." Joel asked her about it. "Well, we'd sort of been hopping all our lives. Or flying. That's what we usually did to get from one place to the other. But walking was like taking on a huge opponent and coming out on the bottom. We fell so many times that it was a wonder that we survived those first few months. Then it was learning to eat. Gross. When I think of all the things that we tried at the beginning. Again, small wonder we're still alive. But walking was the hardest thing to learn. Even learning to fly as a chick wasn't nearly as difficult. Mom just tossed us out of the nest and we would fly or not. But walking? You have to learn to balance, bring your body with you as you move. There is picking up your foot enough to walk and then to step over things. Just a lot to do something that as a human, you just do every day."

"I don't remember not being able to walk. I mean, I didn't, not when I was first born, but even after I learned, none of that is in my memory." Joel laughed as he looked at her. "I'll have to make sure that I pay more attention when we teach our children to walk. That would include Miley."

"I have something else that I'd like to talk to you about. As you've heard, I'm thinking about leaving the toys to Blaze. I might come back to it, but for now, I'm going to do something different. It's charitable work around here, and anywhere else we might be needed." Jude told her that they did that now. "Yes, but this isn't going to be on a grand scale like that. I have an idea to help people who have left their partners. Something along the lines of when we helped transport people during the Underground Railroad's time."

"What do you need from us?" Mercy told Jude that she didn't know as yet, but she would get a list. "All right. I'm going back to work now. And so you know, Miley is going to be working with Blaze for a few months. Not much, I'm to understand, but enough for her to come in when there is a new product that needs testing. I believe that Blaze is going to come and ask you sometime today."

After Jude left them, Mercy asked Joel what he was thinking about. She could tell that he wasn't upset, but just deep in thought. When he smiled at her, she knew that he'd either worked it out on his own or he didn't have any deep thoughts after all.

"You're a very good person. I realized that before today, but it just hit me just how generous the six of you are, and that you're always looking out for others." She asked him what he meant by that. "When you were really pissed off at me, you still made it so that I had some money in the bank. I have a feeling that you also set up the job for me here, as well as the ramp on this house. There are a lot of little things that I just came to realize that you've been doing as well. And then there is this help you're going to do with the people of abused relationships. You won't let anyone but your family know that you've been doing that, will you? Not to mention, I'm sure that you've been doing things like this ever since you came into money."

"One thing that the queen taught us was that just because you have it, whatever it is, you shouldn't be selfish to those who don't. Not just food and housing, but even to sit down and have a meal with the ones you share with. Or invite them to your home for one. She was a good queen. The best, from what I was able to see when we helped. And even when the kingdom that we attacked didn't have any hold over her, it was for the people living under such barbarous, harsh living conditions that she had us attack the king anyway." Joel asked her if she'd left them the kingdom. "Not the walls, but yes, the kingdom. The wealth that she had accumulated was vast. Dante gave a great deal of it to the people who depended on her, and the rest was ours. I'll take you to it one of these days."

"I'd love to just see it all. I mean, it might be fun to find old money, and even treasures." She told him that there were a great many treasures. "Anything you'd like to put in the new house?"

"Perhaps. That's a good idea." Mercy stood up as she continued. "How about we go and have a look at the house? It's not far from here. Miley would be able to go to the same school, and it's close to the library and anything else she'd like to get into."

"Good. Let's go. Should we pick up—?" He looked at the open door then back at her. "I can feel her. Miley, I mean. She's on her way here. How did I do that?"

"You thought of her and needed to know where she was. You can do it with anyone that you've touched. Though I would recommend that you don't think too hard on strangers. That could be a bit tedious for you."

Laughing, the two of them went to the front door just before Miley got out of the car. After telling her where they were going, they all loaded up in their car and made their way over to it. Joel told Miley what he'd just discovered.

"Hey Dad, you need to keep up. I've known that for a couple of days."

Joel teased Miley as they drove to the house. But as soon

as they pulled up in front of it, Mercy knew that this was going to be their home forever.

~*~

Joel wasn't sure what to think about the house. Christ, it was huge. And the fact that it had a large fenced in back yard, a swimming pool to rival ones he'd seen on television at the Olympics, as well as a cook's quarters and stables was enough to make him feel faint of heart. They would get horses, Mercy told him.

Just like that, we'll get some horses. He supposed she knew how to ride them. Joel had only seen them at Christmas time when someone in town would give holiday rides on them. But there had never been any snow, not to mention money, to do such things.

"There are six bedrooms on the second floor and two on the top floor. I'm not sure why, but that's what the reports said. The one down here can be turned into an office. There is also a library on this floor." Mercy looked at Miley. "And for you there is an elevator at the back of the house. It only goes up to the second floor, so for now, you can get up there without any trouble. I thought it would be nice for you to have two of the rooms so that you can have an office-like study of your own." They took the elevator up to the second floor as Mercy continued. "The rooms up here are remodeled, but if you want something different, that wouldn't be any trouble either. I think we'll more than likely use the two upstairs as just guest rooms. I'd like to be here with my family. If that's okay with Joel."

"Yes, that's wonderful. I didn't want to be that far away either. And we can use one of the rooms here for the nursery." Miley was getting more excited everyday about the new baby. They were going to the doctor that specialized in shifters next month to find out all sorts of things. Joel entered one of the rooms along the hall. "I think I found the master."

The room was huge, taking up the space of two of the rooms across the hall from it. There was a bathroom with closets, and windows that looked out over the expansive back yard and pool. Plus, from there he could see the driveway and the horse paddock. He could see himself being master of the manor here. He was laughing when he turned back to Mercy.

"What's out there that you find so funny?" He told her what he'd been thinking about. "Good. And as master of the manor, you get to name the place. It's tradition for a bird to be into her nest, so to speak, to name it. I haven't any idea when that started, but when I was just a chick, we were Falcon Nest. Stupid, I know, but—"

"That's perfect. I love it." She asked him if he was sure. "Yes, we're all falcons here. And I would imagine that any children we have would be as well. So this is perfect. I love you."

Joel was kissing Mercy when he heard the crunch of gravel. He didn't think that he'd ever had hearing as good as he did now. Sometimes it was nice, like now, to know they were having company. But other times, in the middle of the night, he could swear he could hear the wood groaning under the weight of age.

"Someone is here." He asked her if she knew who it was. "You know him. It's your brother. I have no idea how he found us here, but I intend to find out. He's becoming a pain in my ass, just so you know."

"Mine too. Let's go and run him off so we can get things squared away at Falcon's Nest." The more he said the name, the more he liked it. As they made their way past Miley, Joel asked her to stay up here. "I don't know what he has to say, if anything, but I'd rather him not know that you're here with us."

79

"All right, Dad, but I have to tell you, I don't think I like my uncle. He's a pain in the butt." She moved past them to the next room. "If you don't really mind, I think I will take two of the rooms up here. I like having my own space."

They were just coming down the stairs when the doorbell sounded as if it were stuck. Joel knew that it was Saul, trying to make a point of letting them know that he was there. The little fucker was going to get a piece of his mind. And he looked at Mercy as they took the last step down.

"I'm going to deal with him. I'd like to think it was once and for all, but I have a feeling that the only way we're going to be rid of him is with him in prison or dead. And I think I have the perfect spot to bury him. In the pasture so that he can be shit on all the time." Mercy was laughing when he opened the door. "What the fuck do you want? And more importantly, how the hell did you know that we were here? Have you been following us?"

"Of course I have. How else would I know where my brother is living? Are you buying this house? Christ, Joel, if you have that sort of money, surely you can spot me a few thousand bucks. It'll be nice to be able to have some nice things too." Saul tried to push past him, and Joel blocked him. "Aren't you going to invite me in? It's not very nice of you. How will I know where I might be staying should you have me over for dinner or something?"

"You're not going to be invited anywhere where we are. And as for coming in, no. Not on your fucking life. Besides, Saul, there is nothing here for you to steal, so it's a moot point, don't you think?" Saul said he sounded like he was being nasty. "I was hoping you'd get that. And I'm happy to say that I was being nasty to you. I don't want you around. Don't you get that? I have a nice life now, one that I'm very happy with. I have a good wife, a child on the way, and I have a daughter that I love. You, however, are not on any of those lists of things that I love. I want you to get out of my life, now, or you'll be arrested for trespassing."

"You can't do that to me." Joel asked him why not. "I'm your brother, Joel, in the event that it slipped your mind. I'm your blood relative, and therefore, I mean more to you than any of these — these people are nothing compared to what I am to you."

"You've got that all wrong, Saul. You are nothing compared to what I have with them. And you will never be anything more than a pain in my ass. Now, this is the last time that I'm going to tell you — stay out of my life, or so help me, Saul, you'll regret it." He looked over his shoulder and smiled at Mercy. "She's not going to give into you either."

"Do you hear the way that he's talking to me, Mercy? Like he has a right to. How come you're not sharing whatever you got with me? I'm your relative too." Mercy laughed. "You think this is funny? All this shit that he's saying to me? I don't. It's rude, and I won't have it."

"You go on thinking that way, Saul, and I can tell you that you'll only get yourself killed." Mercy came to stand next to him and Joel took her hand. "You have been warned. And the next time you come here, I'll warn you that the gatehouse will be manned, and the guard there will have permission to kill you on site if you try and enter. The fencing around this place is electrified as well, so if I were you, I'd not try that way either."

"You guys will pay for this treatment." The siren sounded just as the police pulled into the driveway. Joel didn't know who had called them in, but he was happy to see them. "You fucking called the cops on me? I tell you, Joel, I'm making a list of shit that I'm going to have to have repayment for. You're getting into some big bucks right now. How about you spot me some of it now and I'll forget this whole thing?"

"Mr. Saul Oliver, you're to come away from the house. Now. You're trespassing." Saul looked at him before turning to the officer. Joel saw hatred there, deeper than he'd ever seen it on his brother before. Officer Allen Windjammer put his hand on his gun and unsnapped it before he spoke again. "You give me any shit and I'll be obliged to shoot you where you stand."

"Such hostility around here." Saul turned back to them again before going down the steps. "I'll be seeing the two of you soon. And that little girl of yours. It'd be a real shame if something happened to her while I'm being treated this way."

"Did you just threaten them?" Allen laughed when he tossed Saul on the car. "You're an idiot, just like I was told. I'm going to take you in and let you stew a while in a cell for what you did. Christ man, do you have any idea how much this couple does for this town? Apparently not. Well, let me fill you in on a thing or two. They've made the jail one of the best in the state. You might want to thank them for making it so you can take a crap in private. There are better foods, as well as things for a prisoner to do while he or she is staying with us."

After reading Saul his rights, Allen put him in the back of the cruiser. Saul could still be heard yelling at him, so Joel tuned him out in order to hear what Allen had to say to them. It looked as if he was trying to find the best way to say it when Mercy spoke.

"Say it before I have to reach down into your throat and pull it out for you. It might be less painful for you for me not to have to do that to you." He asked about the gatehouse. "I'm looking for someone to fill the spot now. If you know anyone, let me know. Also, the fencing around this place has the ability to be electrified, and I'm going to make sure that it's on its highest setting until that jackass is out of town. Or at the very least out of our hair. Also, and you might want to drop a few hints to the rest of the people in your station, Saul Oliver has committed murder. I can't prove it as yet, but we will."

"All right, I can do that. And I might have just the person for the gatehouse. My brother. He's a retired Navy Seal, and isn't adjusting to people well. Perhaps him out there will give him something to do and not have to hang around with a lot of people." Joel said to send him out to the house. "I can do that. His name is Daniel Windjammer. But most people from the service all call him Jammer. I didn't ask, so I don't know."

They were still laughing when the cruiser pulled away. Going to find Miley, they found her in the bedroom she was going to use as a homework room, she called it, writing down the things she was going to need to finish it off. Even before he could ask, Miley turned to Mercy.

"You have an old desk I can have? I'd rather have wood that has no top. What I mean is, I don't want a secretary kind of desk." Mercy said that she knew of two they had in storage. "If you don't mind."

"No. As a matter of fact, we're going to the warehouse after we settle up with the movers tomorrow, I think. I wanted to show your dad around." She asked if she could go. "Of course. There are some old Victorian beds stuck in there someplace, as well as a couple hundred chairs you might want to put in your new room. It wouldn't be any trouble to get them redone for you. I know a guy here in town that loves doing it."

"I'd love to see them. I bet over the years you've kept a lot of that sort of stuff." Joel told Miley that they were going to put a few of the pieces in the house. "That would be way awesome. I have a dream of having a huge family table, and all the aunts around it with their mates. It would be so cool at Christmas."

They decided to go out to dinner, someplace they could splurge on a good steak as well as some wine. They had a driver now; hired by one of the others to drive them instead of them having to find parking spaces. Joel was looking forward to moving into the bigger house and having Christmas there, just like Miley was.

As they were riding down the elevator to the main level, Miley asked about the grounds around the house. Mercy was telling her about the horses that they could get, because there was a great deal of land to ride on. Joel was looking at the large garage with the apartment over the top. He was muddling through wondering if Daniel would like to live there. It would be nice for the added protection, he thought.

It only took them an hour to get to Columbus, and they didn't have to wait long for a seat. Joel was surprised to see that a great many people seemed to know Mercy. She introduced him and Miley as her family to every one of them. Soon they'd have to make it official, but for now, he was content with just having his women near him as much as he could.

Chapter 6

Saul couldn't understand why he was in jail. He'd not actually done anything to the little girl yet. He was pretty sure that just threatening someone couldn't result in jail time. He'd have to look into that when he got out of here. The officer came to get his empty tray just as he was trying to figure out who he could call to come bail him out.

"Hey, you got any friends that would like to make a fast buck? I mean, I'd pay nicely once I'm paid. You know, after the job is done." Joey, he thought his name was, just bent and picked up the tray without answering him. "Are all you cops so stuck up that you'd not answer a man when he asked a polite question?"

"I'm sure that anyone in here wouldn't do a thing for you. But go ahead, tell me what this plan of yours is so I can slap another few days on your sentence." He didn't know for sure if the guy was serious or not, so kept his mouth closed. This was the weirdest jail system he'd ever been in. "I see. So, you might have gotten a clue that to tell a cop your plans, or to say something that could get you into trouble in front of a cop, is a bad idea. I'm glad that we could teach you at least one thing while in here."

"It's considered rude to talk over someone's head." Joey walked away laughing hard at him. "He certainly isn't laughing with me. Mother fucker."

Sitting down on the chair that was nicer than he'd seen in those expensive furniture stores, he wondered yet again what that woman had seen in his brother enough to marry him. Saul supposed his brother was nice—too nice if you asked him. And he wasn't nearly as good looking as Saul was. Joel was a sap too.

Saul thought of himself as a man's man. He had his own definition of that, not being able to find anything under that sort of title in the dictionary. Saul thought of himself as a man who got things done, and damn the consequences. Usually that was what got him into trouble. But what sort of life could you live if you were always worried about getting caught?

Saul had his own way of getting out of things, mostly with the cops. Any of them, from the little local asses, like the ones here, all the way up to the Feds. The big guys were harder to impress with his knowledge of shit going down, but on occasion he'd be able to impress one or two of them. That would get him a *get out of jail on a lesser sentence* card that he usually had to use within days of getting it.

"This is just stupid." Saul usually talked to himself. And when he did, he thought that he gave himself the best answers. When he had a crew, which wasn't that often, he didn't like sharing, so he would bounce ideas off them. It was difficult to get them to agree to his way of doing things, so he usually did it on his own by killing them off and going about his business. Messy, but effective.

Saul would admit to anyone that he was a crook. He took pride in the fact that he'd not worked a job that wasn't a way to get to something he wanted in all his life. When he took a job, it was to get insider information, find someone to let him in after hours, or simply to steal whatever he could walk out with on his first day.

Saul loved stealing. To him, it was a national pastime. People said all the time that they didn't take things. Lies, all of it. People would take a pen here or there. Print up something that was personal on company time, using company paper. He knew that some people would order gifts for the family online or even play games. It was all theft. Every single bit of it. What he never understood was why they thought that he was the criminal and they weren't. Fuckers, every last one of them.

Saul hadn't any idea how long they thought they could hold him here. He had shit to do and things that he had to put into motion. There was the slight worry that they'd be watching him a little closer now. Not that it really worried him that much. Saul had a way to slip in and out of shadows more than most.

When the cop came back, this time he wasn't alone. With him was a fancy man. Had to be a lawyer.

"You my court appointed shithead?" The man shivered and said that he was not. "What do you want? As you can see, I'm kinda busy here."

"I have a proposal for you." Saul told him he wasn't any kind of homo, but thanks all the same. "You're a disgusting man, has anyone ever told you that? I'm here to offer you money to go —"

"I'll take it." The man said nothing as Saul stood up and put out his hand. "Hand it over, Fancy Man. I haven't got all day. How much is it? Enough to get me out of here?"

"You need to shut up and listen. I'm not going to just hand over money to you without telling you what you have to do to get it." Saul sat back down. There was a catch to everything

87

nowadays. "I will pay you ten thousand dollars to leave the country."

"Nope. I'll take the money, but I'm not going anywhere. I know for a fact that my new family has a great deal more than that. This is just a drop in the toilet for them. Why do they want me to leave the country, anyway?" The man told him. "They just want me to leave them alone? That still doesn't answer why I have to leave the country. And besides, ten grand isn't going to get me far with me having to start over, you know."

"Start over? What is it you think you need to replace that you've had before? You have nothing now, from what I've been told about you." Fancy Man snorted at him. "You take the money, leave tonight on the first flight out, and you'll get ten more when you land on the other end. However, you return, and all bets are off, I'm told to tell you."

"You think that is supposed to scare me away? No, it's not going to happen. And even if I wanted to leave the country, I can't. I'm a felon, as you know. I wasn't even supposed to leave the state. But I told them I was coming to see my brother be wedded. The fool. And that got me a free pass for a month." Allen asked him how long ago that was. "Well, I'm not foolish enough to tell you that, now am I?"

"Are you going to do as asked?" Saul just pushed the chair back into the lounging position and closed his eyes. "All right, I'll take that as a no. There is another deal on the table, Mr. Oliver. Are you willing to listen to it?"

"Sure, go ahead." He didn't move, thinking that he'd rattle the man and he'd have to come back. "You go on and tell me what you think I'll do for them."

"Mercy Oliver, your sister-in-law, has said that if you come around her family again, for any reason, then you'll be a dead man."

Saul looked over at the cop, asking if that was a threat.

"No, not a threat when it comes from her about you. I'd say that it was a promise. She will kill you. And when she does, I doubt much that anyone will give a shit." Joey laughed, then he smiled. "You should know that the bodies of your parents are being exhumed. There is a question of someone murdering them. They're pretty sure that it was you, if you didn't get that."

"Who the hell ordered that? That fucking brother of mine? He's a moron. And if there is something like that with their bodies, then he did it." Joey just nodded, and the lawyer cleared his throat. "You tell that bitch that I'm not the least bit worried about her or my brother. I want them to acknowledge me in a financial way, or things might start to fall apart for them. And yes, that was a threat. Fuck this shit. I want my own lawyer. Get me one, doofus."

Joey was laughing again as he walked away with Fancy Man. This shit was just stupid. The fact that everyone seemed to be getting a kick out of his predicament was pissing him off too. And he knew from past experience, being pissed off would get him into trouble. Stupid people lost their cool, not smart ones like him.

When his next tray came around, it was brought to him by none other than his new family member. Mercy sure was a pretty thing. And he'd bet anything Saul could have her begging for mercy in no time. When she pushed his tray under the little opening he just sat there, waiting for her to beg him for something.

"I'm not begging you for anything, you moron. You had your chance. I've come here to ask you if you have your will and such in order." He asked her if she was threatening him. "No. I doubt it would do me any good anyway. I've come here for the very reason I said. Just to make sure that you're not

89

leaving anything undone. I'm not one to make idle threats. I will do just what I said. I will kill you if you bother my family again."

He laughed. Saul couldn't help it. Mercy wasn't any bigger than a bug to him. He might be older than her—he was sure he was—but he was also stronger, and he was a man. When she laughed, he asked her what she thought was so funny.

"You are, if you think that you having a dick will make a difference when you come up against me. I'm much stronger than I look." He asked her if she could read his mind. "I can. And I have a feeling that any moron with an IQ the size of a gold fish would be able to read it too. You must be so much fun at poker."

"What the hell do you think you can do to me, little girl? And I'll do as I wish, when I want. You have money and I want it." She said nothing but looked up at the camera that hung at the end of the hall. When it popped and sizzled, he watched as the second one, at the other end, did the same thing. "So? You have a bit of magic. Most people do."

"Do they? Can they do this?" She shifted into a bird. Not one of those cute ones he was forever seeing on television, but one that looked like it could snap him in half with her beak, and then swallow him down without a thought. Even her head, bent to accommodate its size compared to the height of the ceiling, was bigger than him. Saul leapt back from it, and she laughed when she became a person again. "Did I scare you? I fucking hope so."

"How did you do that?" She just smiled at him and then snapped her fingers. Both cameras buzzed for a moment, and he'd bet anything that they had come back on. "I demand that you tell me how you did that. Do you have any idea how much fucking money we can make off a show of you? Christ, people would pay big bucks to see you do that. And the Feds would never arrest me again, even if I were to take out a gun and kill the president. Just because of the uses that they could find for you and that bird."

"You really are stupid, aren't you? Do you have any...? Well, I'd say you've not thought beyond what you can get out of something for nothing your entire life. I cannot believe that you and Joel are from the same gene pool. He's the sweetest most generous man I've ever met. While you? You're nothing but a money-grubbing ass wipe that only looks for what things can get him." She shook her head as she continued. "The threat still stands. You come near my family, in any way, shape, or form, and I will pick you up in my claws, fly as high as I can, and drop you. There will be nothing left of you but a stain on the dirt." She was suddenly in his face, coming through the cell bars, his body lifted from the floor. "You will die, Saul Oliver, and trust me when I tell you, I will enjoy it more than you can believe."

After she dropped him to the floor, he sat there as she faded from the cell. Saul didn't get up right away, his body still trembling from the encounter. But the longer he sat there, thinking, the more ideas he came up with on how to get more than just money out of her talents. Saul was sure that he'd be on easy street for the rest of his life.

Laughing, he got up. Taking his tray to the little table that was cemented to the floor, he laughed harder. The things that he was going to get from this were going be the best scheme he'd ever done. Pulling off the cover from his plate, Saul screamed. The little birds, all of them the color of blood, came shooting up off his plate and slammed him in the face.

Falling back, waving to keep them from pecking his eyes out, the chair tumbled, and he fell back. The last thing that Saul remembered thinking was her laughable attempt at getting him to back off.

~*~

As soon as she left the station house, Mercy took to the skies. She was just angry enough to go back to the jail, tear a hole in the side of the place, and grab Saul up to do just as she said she would. It was small wonder to her that she'd not killed him when she had the chance. Instead, like a fool, she feared she had given him yet another chance to try and hurt one of them.

I can actually feel your anger. Wow, you must be about as pissed off as I've ever known anyone to be. She told Joel what had happened, leaving nothing out. *Well, I hate to say this, but it's nothing more than you expected from him, correct?*

I guess. But he was actually giddy about me shifting instead of being fearful of what I could do to him. Even going so far as to try and think up ways to make a few bucks off me. Joel said he was sorry. *Don't be. He's the one that should be sorry. I'm not going to hold back on him when he tries his shit.*

I was thinking about joining you in the sky. That made her anger turn to something so profoundly different, she begged him to join her. *I'm not sure how good I'll be at this. I mean, the little bit of practice that I've had, it didn't go that well.*

You were too worried about looking stupid. I told you, we all had to learn how to do what you do every day. Walking is much harder than it looks. She saw him below her. Miley was sitting on the deck in a lounge chair with a blanket over her legs. As soon as her dad shifted, she clapped loud enough for Mercy to hear. *Just think of flying, Joel, and come join me in the skies.*

They had discovered that not only could he be a falcon like her, but he could also turn into her larger falcon. Like the one she'd been that destroyed castles and saved their people. She had enjoyed watching him struggle with bouncing along the grass, trying to walk. And her and Miley had had a good time trying to get him to flap his wings. It was like watching a comedy of errors with him. But he'd been so good natured about it that Mercy had loved him all the more for it.

When he struggled again with liftoff, Mercy waited. He'd get it or not. But she already felt better than she had before simply because he loved her, and her him. They were perfectly suited, she thought.

Joel did much better than she thought he would once he got up and going. The lift, she'd told him, would be the most difficult to master. But once a person had that, things like flapping their wings would come to them easier. As soon as Joel soared by her, she laughed, feeling like a great weight had been lifted from her heart.

This is beautiful. Look at the tops of the trees. The way they sway and move is amazing. She let him see what she'd not for a long time—her age and jadedness had made her forget the beauty beneath her. *Oh, Mercy. This is why you do this for blowing off steam, isn't it?*

Even before becoming a human, she had long since only seen things in the form of strategy, how to best make trees or boulders work for her. How the terrain was laying in the direction of the waterways. She and the others had gotten good at making things work for them. Saving lives and the kingdom had become their first priority. And in turn, it kept them all alive to fight another day.

They played in the skies until well after dark. It didn't matter to them, being predators, that the darkness would bring out creatures that only ate at night. They were meaner, sharper at getting in and out of situations. And they could soar in and out of danger better than most. Mercy showed him how to ride the currents.

When they landed, they noticed the time was after midnight. Miley had long since gone to bed, Dutch told them, and left them out a tray of food, telling them that the hot tub had been delivered earlier that day and was now up to temperature. There was just enough chill in the night air to make the sound of getting into the tub tempting.

Sliding into the steaming heat, they both moaned. Mercy felt his moan all the way to her core, but she was much too relaxed and very happy to be turned down if it was only just the tub giving him such pleasure. But she should have known better. Almost as soon as the thought was out of her head, he reached for her.

His callused hands were tender. Joel's strong fingers massaged in places that the heated water couldn't touch. As he worked over her muscles, she sat facing him on his lap. Leaning into his neck, resting her chin on the edge of the tub, she let him have his way with her.

"You are much too tense to have just been soaring over the land, my love. You aren't still thinking of Saul, are you? If so, then get his rattlesnake meanness out of your head and think of me. And all the things that I plan to do to you." She told him there was nothing on her mind. "Good. I'm going to tell you something, and I want you to remember. I love you very much, and that's the reason that I've gone ahead and done this. I've set us up to be married in the morning. Miley helped me pick out the flowers and the people that we would both want there when we tie the knot."

"Why would you...? Oh, yes, that's the right place. I'm not upset about that. I'm glad you did it. You're making me so weak with this that I might have to spend the night here." He laughed softly, his hands and fingers never stopping their treatment to her body. "What time? And I have the perfect dress picked out already. It's nearly — Holy shit, that's where it aches."

He massaged that area until she cried out that she was

finished. It felt so good that she told him that it had been about as good as sex. Joel pulled her head up and looked at her. She could see it there — she'd just laid down a challenge to him.

When he lifted her up, Mercy thought that he was going to set her aside. But when he brought her down over his cock, his hand sliding over her pussy as he held himself for her, she cried out. He was harder than she'd thought he'd be just for touching her skin.

"You make me hard by just breathing in my direction, love. You mean everything to me, and I want you every day." She moved, sliding forward and back as he played with her breasts. "I love the way your breasts feel in my hands. How they fill my palms up, spill over my fingers. And the tightness of your nipples makes me want to beg you to let me suckle them."

He did that, taking just the tips of her breasts into his mouth one at a time and nibbling on them until she was begging him to take her. To make her come. But he was relentless in making her suffer. She rode him faster, harder, but he never once gave her what she wanted most of all — to scream out her release in a way that made her throat sore for several hours afterwards.

Joel teased her, played with her body until she was ready to scream for an entirely different reason. She was tense, then relaxed. Her body like a live wire, then soft and relaxed. Mercy begged him, pleaded with him, and at one point even threatened him. All he did was laugh softly, telling her to wait. She no longer wanted to wait. Mercy needed him now.

"You want to come?" She cried, no longer able to say anything, her need was so high. "Come for me, baby, and I'll fuck you hard again."

She screamed, her body no longer able to hold back when he pinched her clit. As soon as her body hit the peak he pressed against her again, and her body bowed back as the next and then the next climax took her under. Joel bit into her breast and Mercy came again, her body coming apart and slamming back together so many times that she didn't know if she'd survive it all.

Weak with her releases, she nearly begged him again, this time to let her go, when he picked her up with his cock still buried in her body and laid her over the decking around the tub. He fucked her this way, her body spread out before him as he pounded her hard. And even though she thought she was finished, that she couldn't take anymore, she came again when he released his hot cum into her.

Stars danced behind her eyelids. Mercy saw her life, all of it, flash before her eyes. And when she thought she was dead, her body simply no longer able to sustain itself, she came again.

Mercy woke, not even realizing that she'd fainted, in their bed. Joel was beside her, talking softly to her. It took her a moment to realize that he was telling her how much he loved her, how he would never be able to show her just how much. Mercy turned to him, and he smiled.

"You fainted." She nodded, curling her body around his. "I thought for sure that I'd killed you. I mean, you might be immortal, but that was intense."

"No kidding. I don't think I will survive if you have a mind to do that too often." He laughed with her. Mercy looked up at him. "I love you so much, Joel. I never would have believed that after all these years, I'd be able to find someone that could make me want to be in love. You have surpassed everything that I could have hoped for in looking for a mate."

"And tomorrow, I make you my wife. After all this time for me, I only thought that I'd be with Miley, her being my rock, my foundation. I never knew until I fell in love with you that a person could love two people so much." He put his hand on her flat belly. "And now, I have another person that not only do I love, but as much as I can love anyone."

She rested her head on his chest and listened to his heart beating. It was like a ticking clock, strong and solid. Closing her eyes, Mercy smiled. It had been a very long time since she'd felt this way — in love, loved, and happy.

The dream was one that she'd never had before. It was where the castle had been, the walls of it still standing tall, the people surrounding it working their fields and hanging out the wash. As she drew closer to the scene, not sure why she'd dream such a dream, she saw a woman. It took her several moments to realize that it was Dante, her queen.

Landing on the fence post, only then realizing that she was a bird, she watched as a woman in the yard was handed a bundle by Dante. The queen looked right at Mercy but didn't seem to know who or what she was to her.

It hit her in that moment that she'd never met her. The queen hadn't used her magic, hadn't changed her into what she would later need. And the bundle was a child, small and not yet cleaned of his birth.

"You will care for him for me?" The woman, young and with a child of her own in the basket at her feet, nodded. "I will care for you and him forever, Mary. But you must never tell a soul who he is. For it will mean his death should the bad king die."

"I will care for him like my own. The coin you give me, it will help all of us in ways that you will not know." Dante told her that she would know and was happy for the help. "Nay, my lady. I know what this means to you. And you have given me a great honor. I will care for him for you. Keep him safe as well."

Dante moved away after thanking the woman. Mary.

97

Mercy remembered a woman named Mary who had been one of the first to be moved, her and her two children. Mercy remembered the face too. She was young and well cared for, and she was an immortal. Mercy knew that she was to find the child, because the child of her queen would be her king.

Chapter 7

Saul had been released just that morning and made his way to the hotel where he had been staying. It was old and abandoned, and it stank, but he had a roof over his head for the most part and running water. It was cold, sure, but it wasn't too bad.

He'd have to find himself something before winter. If he didn't, someone would come out and find him a popsicle one day. Laughing at his own joke, he found that his clothing was still there, but it had a smell to it, like some animal had pissed all over it.

"Fucking wild animals."

His mind went to the woman, Mercy, and he shivered. She was one of them fucking shifter things. Not that he was afraid of her. She was a bird, by God, and he knew all he'd need to do to take her out was to kill her. A little bird or a big one, it would die by his hand soon.

After taking his clothing to the sink, he washed them up with the little bars of soap that he'd found when rummaging around. There had been cases of the soap, shampoo, and toilet paper. With the running water, the toilets could be flushed with a bucket, so Saul considered himself lucky on that. He was able to take a good shit and wash it all away.

The bed was lumpy. Even with several of the mattresses that he'd gathered up, he would still wake with a spring in his ass — or in other soft places on his body. Once, he'd had a spring cut him in the belly. But the people at the jail, they'd fixed it up for him. Didn't want him to die on their watch, they'd told him. Another fucking bunch, Saul thought.

Just as he'd been leaving, Allen came to tell him that his parents, both of them, had been exhumed. He wasn't really worried about that too much. He had bigger fish to fry, so to speak. By the time they figured out he'd killed Dad, and then found the poison in Mom — if there were any traces of it left — he'd have himself some cash and be hidden away for good.

He'd thought there was money. Saul had seen his parents with all sorts of new things. Then there was the big motor home. They'd never camped a day in their life as far as he knew, but they were getting the big rig all filled up to go on a trip. Christ, had he only known then that they'd gotten it really cheap, he could have killed them both at the same time. The thing might well have blown up on them. Had a blow out on a tire or something like that. Instead, he'd had to kill off one of them to get the other to talk. And there was nothing.

They'd lost the house; his mom had told him in her grief. Lost it all because they'd not been able to keep up with the payments. The motor home, a thirty-year-old sucker, had had more wrong with it than was fixed, but they were excited to have something to live in when the house was taken by the bank.

"We tried and tried to get some money to pay the payments, but we didn't have the things we thought we had to sell off." His mom had looked at him; all signs of being grief stricken over Dad were gone. "You took them, didn't you, Saul? Whatever you did with them, I do hope you got a fair price for them. Because of you, we were going to be homeless. Those were our nest egg, and you stole them from us."

Apparently, his parents had been hording antiques, coins, and old smelly baskets to sell off when they'd gotten older. Yes, he had stolen them. And after finding out what some of the pieces were worth, he was going to find the man he'd sold them to and kill him. The dealer had given him nothing compared to what he should have gotten.

Mom cried for a bit more, and he told her to drink her tea. It was laced with poison, much more than he should have given her all at once, but he'd been pissed off and wanted her to pay. Fucking bullshit. No money? He wished he could dig her up and kill her all over again, and his father.

His dad had been hard to kill off. Saul had been feeding him the poison in the candy that he loved—an entire four-pound box of chocolates just for him. But after eating only a couple of them, his dad had tossed them out, saying they were tainted. Dad had known what Saul had been up to. So he'd gone outside with him when he'd been gathering wood for the fireplace, and hit him in the head with the axe. No more waiting for him to die off.

Mom had blamed him for Dad's death immediately after finding his cold body. Saul had only stuck around to see the reaction on Mom's face when she found Dad. But she'd looked right up at him and pointed her finger at him to blame it all on him. There wasn't any way that he could convince her that she was insane for thinking that. She'd even told the police that she thought he'd done it.

"There isn't any way that my husband fell on that axe, Officer. He was very good at putting it back with the blade protector on it. He paid thirty dollars for that thing, and he made sure it was used every single time after cutting wood." The officer glanced at Saul and told Mom that perhaps he'd forgotten. "No, he was always good at it, as I said. He never wanted any of the kids, ours included, to be able to fall on it or take it for whatever reason. My son here did it to him. For whatever reason, Saul killed him off. And now I'm worried that he could be coming after me next."

The officer had taken him aside. "If I find out that you killed your father, Saul, I'll come after you myself. That was a good man there, and if you ended his life for no reason other than you could, then you'll regret it. I promise you."

Saul had learned to have a face that no one could read. It had served him very well over the years before that day, and since. All he did was stare at the man, looked at him straight in the eye as if he had nothing at all to fear from him. And he didn't. No one frightened him.

Mercy did. She scared the shit out of him. And he knew better than to try and take her as someone that he'd hold for ransom. Nor would he take Joel. He'd be hell bent to stay with Mercy, and she might well come after Saul just for him taking Joel.

It would have to be the child. First of all, she'd cause him no trouble. Lifting her out of that chair might be hard; she could be heavy from just sitting on her ass all the time. Saul was sure that he'd be able to manage it. And after he killed her—and he would, no matter what—what would she need with the wheelchair anyway? She wouldn't.

He'd been holding onto the newspapers that he'd found all over the place here. They were outdated, of course, but he really wasn't going for anything to read. He wanted them to wrap her body in. The shower curtains had all been stolen away, he'd seen, so Saul had to improvise.

The previous owners had even done him a solid by not

filling in the holes from when the gasoline tanks had been taken out. Even the big earth mover was sitting there ready to use. Saul hadn't ever driven one before, wasn't even sure this one worked, but it would go a long way in making sure the kid didn't have animals dragging her body off when he was done with her. If it didn't—oh well, she'd just be part of something's dinner.

Saul didn't have a plan. He'd never been one to work things out before he did them. He was more of a wing-it sort of person. Sometimes it even worked in his favor for not having anything set in stone. Most of the time, especially of late, he would have to wing-it all the way to the end. Which, he surmised, had served him well too. No one knew the plan any better than he did, so he didn't have to worry about someone fucking him over.

Laughing, he decided that he needed something to eat other than candy bars. The day before he'd been arrested, Saul had found a vending machine and had busted it open. Everything in it had been expired, and it wasn't until he'd eaten two of the candy bars that he noticed that some rat, the four-legged kind, had gotten to them.

Cutting off the chewed-up part had become tedious, so he started biting around their bite marks. He'd forget to look where he was biting sometimes, but all in all, it had filled his belly. But it was making him slightly ill, the sugary diet, and he thought about walking into town to get a meal.

Saul wasn't sure how he was going to get his meal—he only had about four cents on him. At the police station he'd tried to claim that they'd taken the ten he had in his wallet, but that hadn't panned out. They had a digital recording of what they'd taken from him, including taking a picture of the contents of his wallet.

"People are so distrusting nowadays."

103

Laughing at his own little joke, he walked along the highway towards town. It wasn't that far, hardly a mile, but he hated walking all the same. He was just about to leap off the road to avoid an oncoming car when he saw who it was. His brother was coming toward him in a brand new car. Flagging him down, he was surprised when Joel didn't run him down.

"You out looking for me?"

Joel didn't say anything, just handed him a grocery bag full of food. Then when he got the second one from his brother, Joel just drove on. After turning around in the parking lot where he was staying, Saul watched him just drive away. Like they were just a couple of people sharing the same road.

Going back to the hotel, he looked over what he had. Saul wasn't sure if he'd poison him or not, so he took extra care in looking things over. Everything was sealed up, but that didn't mean shit when it came to the availability of syringes nowadays. Saul even shook up the water bottles, making sure they didn't have a leak in them, before he sat them aside.

"Water just isn't going to cut it, Joel. You should know that a man like me would need something stronger." Laughing, he set the cans of food on the table as he wondered how Joel thought he was going to cook the stuff. It wasn't until he was at the bottom of the second sack that he realized that he'd sent him some canned heat. "Well, if that don't beat all. Didn't even know they made sterno cans anymore."

With the can opener he'd unearthed too, Saul sat about making himself a nice dinner. There was a can of meat too, some sort of stew stuff, and lots of vegetables. While he normally wouldn't have touched the things, he was hungry enough to eat them too.

After stuffing himself on all the contents of both bags, he looked around for a note from Joel. Surely, he'd let him know that he was on his side in this. Or at the very least, let him know when he was coming back with more food. Nothing. Not even a phone number he could call him on.

"What is this world coming to? A man can't even call his own brother up and ask him when's a good time to kidnap his daughter?" Laughing harder, he laid back down on the bed. He really had worn himself out, walking that little bit of a way, and realized that he'd have to start taking better care of himself.

The girl was going to be his biggest payday yet. He hadn't any idea how much to ask for, but it was going to be at the very least a million bucks. It might be more, then he'd come down if they said they didn't have it. But at least that much, and he would be happy with his work.

Not satisfied. Never that. He liked money and the things that he could buy with it. And how it made him feel when he could flash it around like he had it all. It was seldom that Saul was with a lot of cash. Usually he just had a twenty or a fifty when he was really lucky. Then he'd wrap it around a bunch of ones. Or sometimes when he was really strapped, he'd just have it around a bunch of paper. Usually didn't work well, but he could fool a few chumps.

Closing his eyes, all that Saul could think about was coming into his money. One way or another, he was going to get a piece of the pie. Hell, he thought with a laugh, he might just take the whole fucking thing. Turning over, the springs caught him just as he was moving and tore a long scratch in his back. Damn it all to hell, he was going to make the girl pay for this.

~*~

Mercy knew what was going to happen. At least she had a good idea what was going to go down. Saul was going to try and take Miley, and Mercy decided that she might just let him. Justified homicide would make her feel pretty good about

105

killing the bastard. Mercy looked up when Piper entered her office.

"I got the reports back on the bodies. Did you know that he'd demanded that they both be cremated, and then him have the ashes? Right now I'm still trying to figure out why they didn't consult Joel on the decisions. Not that it mattered in the long run. The only reason that Saul wasn't able to cremate them is because his parents had filled out their final arrangements a few years ago and didn't want to be burned to death. Their words, not mine." They laughed a little. "She was poisoned, no doubt about that. There was enough in her system at the time of death to have killed an elephant. Also, there were traces of it found in his father's body. I guess it wasn't working fast enough for him, and he hit him with the axe. No one, not in all this time, was able to find the murder weapon until the day before yesterday. It had been in the back of the shed under so much shit that it was small wonder I was able to find it after you told me where to look."

"He has a lot of misdeeds in his mind that I'm going to start looking into. Well, have others look into. Joey has a list of things that he's sharing with New Mexico. And there are other deaths that he's had his hand in. The problem with some of them is it'll be hard to pin them on him. I've come to realize that the man can be like a fart in the wind when it's necessary. What did you find out about the will?" Piper said that there had been one, but it had been voided. "Because of no money."

"Pretty much. I did have someone look into seeing what it would take to get the house back for Joel, but it's not going to happen, I'm afraid. The house was torn down in the name of progress. Progress that only went as far as tearing down an entire block of houses, then doing nothing else. The only thing left was this little shack, for some reason. I think it sat too far back off the road. Lack of funding, I was told, stopped the entire project. Anyway, there are a few possessions that I was able to get. The bank took them in order to sell them off for back payments. That never happened either. They'd been behind in their payments for years, but only by one. And then about two years ago, the bank, pressured by the people that wanted the improvement, decided to toss them out. It wasn't anything that Joel's parents hadn't expected to happen. The banker, a semi nice guy, told them monthly that it could well happen."

"What did Saul do about the house once they were gone? I mean, did he live there long enough to make some money off their things?" Piper said that he'd pretty much sold off everything of value before he killed them. "So, the bank had nothing to use to catch them up. That guy is a peach."

"Mom and Dad had a lot of valuable antiques. A lot of them worth thousands of dollars. They were holding onto them to pave their way into a smaller house someday, and have it paid for so that there would be nothing they'd have to worry about." Joel kissed her on the mouth and hugged Piper before continuing. "Mom called me a couple of months before she was killed. She told me that it was all gone. All the books, first editions that they'd paid nothing much for. Swords that they'd picked up at estate sales that the auctioneer had no idea what they were. Things like that. Oh, and they had art too, some of it from extremely famous artists. Saul found it, sold it off for more than likely nothing much, and they were left without anything to fall back on."

"You do realize that all this is going to hit him at once, don't you? I mean, once the yarn starts to unravel around him, he's going to be put away for a long time. And if he touches Miley.... Well, we'll take care that he pays as well." Piper looked at her, then back at Joel as she explained to him what she'd found on his parents' bodies. "I'm so sorry, Joel.

107

But I have a feeling that you might have known about this anyway, correct?"

"Yes, I suspected it, but hearing that he did murder them both makes it no less difficult." He looked away before saying anything else. "I was going to take Miley to see them the summer they were murdered. It was going to be a long trip for her — she didn't travel well even for the few hours that it would have taken to get there. But they only got to see her once, when she was just a little girl."

"I'm so sorry, Joel." He nodded and stood up. "Did you need help with the interview today? I'm sure that any one of us can quiz you on what to ask."

"I got it." Joel kissed Mercy again and told Piper he'd see her later. But he stopped at the door just before leaving the room and turned back to Mercy. "This position that I'm hiring someone for, I need to know if you plan to interview them as well."

"No, I don't think that'll be necessary. If you think this man is good for the job, then I'm all for it." Joel left them then and Piper asked what was going on. "The school board is short two members. Joel said that he'd take one of the positions if he was allowed to hire the second one. I think he had it in his mind to have the pack leader be a part of it anyway. This way, the pack will have a say in what goes on with their own kids in the school."

"What happened to the other members, or do I want to know?" Mercy told her. "Christ. You mean they were taking the school funding for three years and no one caught on until now? How is that even possible?"

"Joel found it. He was looking over some of the books — I haven't any idea why — and noticed that there were large sums of money missing at the end of each year. Also, and this is what caught his attention first, the petty cash was nearly half a million dollars. There was never that much in the way of money in it, but it never had to be checked until it went below two hundred and fifty thousand. Since it never did, according to their records, no one noticed."

"He's been looking into a few other things for us too, did you know that?" Mercy told her that he loved numbers. "I can see that. He has the mind of a brilliant man. Joel also found out that the pack was being charged more interest than other people at the bank. And that they weren't allowed to charge things to an account at the grocery store like the humans were. After he told me, I had Jude go in and make sure that they didn't do that again. Blaze took care of the banker. And no, before you ask, she didn't kill him. But for a while there, I guess it was a little close."

Piper said she was going to put Joel in charge of the books for her business. She wasn't having any trouble, but it would be one less thing she had to worry about. Mercy said that he'd love that, to feel useful.

"Well, you might want to talk to him about paying him. He seems to think that us paying him for working for us is wrong. I told him how it would help on taxes, and he isn't budging. I thought about telling him to donate it to some worthy cause, but I wanted to talk to you about it first. How about a trust? Set up for kids that need chairs, ramps on their homes, and things like that. Adults too, if necessary. But I think we, after seeing how Miley struggles in places, can make a huge difference in some peoples' lives."

"Tell him that. I think he'd be right on board with that." She said she'd talk to him later then. "Also, Piper, I've been thinking of taking him to see the stash. I was wondering if you guys wanted to go with us. I've decided that I'd like to bring some of the pieces here to put in our home. Miley might like some of it too, to put in her room."

109

"I'd love that. And I've been thinking of getting a home too. I'm sick of apartment life." Mercy said that she had been as well. "If you don't mind, I'm having a meeting with Jude and Esme today. I'll let them know and see if they want to head there as well."

"All right. Great. Let me know." Piper said she would and that she had four pieces to finish up but would be around if she needed her.

Mercy bent over the leather-bound books that she'd been given when Dante had changed them. Mercy was trying to make sense of it all.

The notes that she'd been left from Dante never mentioned a child. However, it did talk about money being paid to someone by the name of Mary. Surnames weren't a thing back then, she was simply Mary the gardener. The sum wasn't a great deal by today's standards, but back then, it would have been a fortune.

There were records too. Of the move, what people were given coins to live on for a time. She wrote of the magic that she'd bestowed on a few of the merchants in the new town. And what was going to be paid to them from the stash they had. Mercy didn't know how that had worked out, as they were never told of paying anyone.

There were other notations as well. A woman by the name of Sally had been made a baker. The one that had been in the castle had died a few days before the great move. That was what it was called too, the great move.

Just as she was closing up the first of many notebooks, she found a notation that she'd not noticed before. It was written in Latin, perhaps so that no one would be able to read it. But Mercy could and sat back as the words sank into her mind.

"My son will be mated to one of my birds." The queen's son? And which one of the others could it be? And where had he been in all this time?

Mercy knew that it couldn't have been Joel. He wasn't an immortal when she met him. And as far as she knew, he wasn't related at all to Dante. Where was this son of the king and queen? What was he doing all this time?

Perhaps he was the one that was paying the woman who had raised him. He would know, she supposed, that there was a stash. And since he'd been born before any of them had been magically changed, he'd be older than them. By how much, Mercy didn't know.

The more information she found, the less she understood. Like for instance, why not tell the king that he had a son? And how had she hidden the pregnancy from him? Had he already been dead when she had the child? Who else knew of him? Mercy had no idea where to go from here, other than to pay more attention to the Latin on the pages.

Starting at the beginning of the book, the first one she'd read, she found other notations about the boy. He was born five months after the king's death. Also, and this one had surprised her, his name was Duncan Neal Dante. No title was attached to his name at this point, but he would be King of Duncan Castle, Lord of the Realm.

Chapter 8

Saul waited outside the hotel off and on for two days. Nothing. Not even a bottle of water from Joel. What the hell was he thinking?

"He's not, that's what he's doing. Not thinking of me out here all by myself without nary a drink and nothing to fill by belly." If he wasn't going to do it all the time, Saul thought to himself, he shouldn't have started it. "Bastard."

But he did have a plan in place now. He knew just where the kid was every Monday and Wednesday. She was driven right by his place on her way to the hospital. Saul figured that she'd need to be cleaned out or something. He didn't know what was wrong with her, other than she was in a chair all the time, but he figured that no one would want to clean up her mess she'd have to be making in that chair all the time.

Looking out the broken window frame, he looked at his cell phone when she went by. She'd be back by this way in two hours and ten minutes. Saul had it all planned out, too. He just needed a gun. And he had until Wednesday to find one. Then things would start looking up for him.

When his brother didn't show up for the fifth day in a

row, Saul made his way into town. He had a few bucks now. It hadn't occurred to him to rob the vending machine of the coins in it. The only problem with the money he had on him was that it weighed his pants down. And with him not having much in the way of a decent meal in a while, his pants no longer fit as they had before. He figured that he'd lost a good thirty pounds, weight that he could barely afford.

The walk did him some good, he supposed. He found an apple tree right off the road that was full of the nice ripe fruit. Also, there was a peach tree, he thought, but there wasn't anything on it worth the trouble. The fruit was about as big as one of the quarters in his pocket, and hard as a stone.

"All this eating of good things is sure making me cleaned out too." Laughing at his own little joke, he thought of what his body had been up to the last week or so.

Saul had noticed that he was abundantly thirsty all the time. It made him glad that he'd saved one of the water bottles that Joel had brought him, so that he could carry it around all the time.

His vision was messing up too. Just last night he'd not even been able to see the article on the newspapers he'd been spreading out for the kid. He was going to have to get that checked out before long, he told himself.

Turning his back to the road, he thought of how much he was peeing lately. And how he figured that it was due to the drinking water all the time. But damn, getting up in the middle of the night to take a piss was annoying as hell.

While he was standing there, he tried to think if he should bother with wearing his shoes all the time. He was forever trying to rub the tingling in them out. Not sure what that meant either, he wanted to rip his shoes off right now and sit there on the cold ground and massage them. He figured it had something to do with the food that Joel had given him.

He'd given him some kind of poison or something, Saul just knew it.

Having to stop all the time to get to his feet was annoying the shit out of him. But he went on, knowing that he had to get himself a gun to take care of the girl and to get money from Joel. He'd hand it over too, if he thought that he'd get his child back. Saul wasn't going to be around when Joel figured out that he'd killed the kid.

"He should think of it as me doing him a favor." Saul would have if he'd been saddled with a cripple. Joel had never mentioned having a child, not in all the years he'd tried to get him to go into business with him. Of course, none of those had panned out, but he was always hopeful that one day he'd make it. And this was going to put him at the top of his game.

Finally getting to the town, he sat down on one of the benches and rubbed his feet once again. He had noticed that his hands were taking on the odor of his feet, and that made him slightly ill. But there wasn't any way that he'd be able to walk at all if he didn't rub them down once in a while.

People hurried by him, and he wasn't proud of that. He was a grown fucking man sitting on a bench in too baggy pants and with his shoes off. Saul was sure that his hair was out of kilter, and he needed to shave off the month long growth that he'd acquired. In a word, he was a mess. A haggard mess, as a matter of fact.

Putting his shoe on was harder than it had been. He was dizzy — he attributed that to not eating today — and he needed to pee. Saul thought that he could drink an entire ocean right now, but all he had was an empty bottle.

"Excuse me. I need to find something to drink. Can you tell me where the closest shop is?" The woman didn't even give him a second glance as she hurried by him. "Listen, bitch. I was nice to you. The least you could have done was say something."

He staggered to the store, which wasn't that far away. As he stumbled into the shop, he stubbed his toe on the rack displaying some kind of Christmas shit. His foot felt like he'd rammed a rod into it. Going to the refrigerator section in the back, he pulled out the first drink he could touch and drank it straight down.

"You have to pay for that." He pulled out a fistful of quarters and dimes and shoved it at the man as he pulled out a second, then a third drink. "Christ, mister, you been in the desert? And I don't know your name. Get it? I made a funny."

"Yeah, you're a funny guy. How much money do I have left after drinking these four drinks? And do you have any juice? I could use a big glass of orange juice right now." He told him only what was in the fridge. He told him how much he'd spent and how much more he had in his hand.

Saul thought about just walking out, but that would mean that he'd not have a thing to drink after this. And he needed a drink like he needed his next breath. His foot wasn't hurting anymore, but he did glance down at it. He thought he must have spilled something on his shoe, as it was stained now.

"You can get two more because they're on special. And if you get six, which I'm guessing you will, they'll be cheaper." He said that he'd take six now and six as he was leaving. After getting the total, he counted out the change and left with his six pops and his empty bottle of water. Saul had forty-five cents left and was still thirsty as fuck.

"You don't look so good, Saul." He stared at the person that spoke without any idea who it was, much less if they were male or female. "It's Remi. I'm one of the sisters to Mercy. I don't think you're well."

"I'm thirsty. Like I'm dying thirsty." She said that she could see that. "And I need to pee all the time. I don't know what is wrong with me."

"I'm calling an ambulance." He told her not to bother, it was probably poison from his brother. "Joel? He'd never do something like that. That's more along your lines, killing people off. At least sit down."

He thought that he had been sitting. Looking around, he saw that he'd drawn a crowd now, something that he hated more than being ill. He looked at the woman again when she asked if she could call an ambulance.

"I told you no. I'm going to be all right. I got shit to do today, and it doesn't matter that I'm a little under the weather right now." He couldn't make out her face or what she was currently doing, but Saul stood up and held onto the wall of the shop for support. "See? I'm just fine. Go on away from here and leave me alone."

Brave words, he realized a few minutes later when he didn't even know where he was. Or for that matter, how he was going to get back to his hotel. But he needed a gun, and he had to find someone that could help him.

Saul had no idea how long he walked around the town. He knew that he'd stopped a few times to massage his feet and to take a leak. Twice he'd been told that he was exposing himself to others, but at this point, he could have been taking his dick out in front of the king of the world and he'd not care. He was aching like he'd never been before.

"Saul?" He turned at the sound of the voice. It was familiar, but he couldn't place the face. "It's Joel. You're sick. Let me take you to the hospital."

"I'm sure you will too. And on the way, you'll put a bullet in my head." He laughed and nearly knocked himself off his feet with it. "I'm just fucking fine. Unless you have a lot of money for me, or a gun, then I want you to get out of my way. You've done enough for me, I'm thinking."

"Did you know that you're bleeding?" He didn't but told his brother that it was none of his concern. "All right. If that's what you want. But you should know that the police are watching you. So, if you really are looking for a gun, then you're not going to have any luck with that. There isn't anyone around you that would sell you a stick of gum for the way you're being watched."

Joel left him. The only way Saul knew that was because his laughter was floating away. That's what all the sounds sounded like now, floating. The cars driving by him sounded the loudest, and people talking, that sounded far away. He didn't know what they were saying, but he could hear them.

Turning back the way he'd come, he paused at a pole, thinking it was a street sign, and called out to the cops. One of them would surely help him return to his home so he could rest.

"I need some help. I'm all turned around. If one of you pricks would point me in the direction of the abandoned hotel down out of town, I'd surely appreciate it." The snickering told him it was Allen. His scent, whatever it was, hit him too. "Why aren't you out taking care of the good citizens of your little podunk town?"

"Why aren't you in prison?" Saul told him that he had been, and wasn't returning. "You think not? Well, I'd rethink that if I were you. Mercy has found a great many crimes that you've not been tried for. Come on, let me get you in the car and I'll take you to your hotel."

Saul could have sobbed with relief when he sat in the warm car. He was cold too, he realized, and wondered at not just the time, but the date. New Mexico had been blazing hot compared to this hell hole.

"You can't stay here; you know that, don't you? First of all, there isn't any running water and electric." Saul told him that there was water. "All right, but no electric. I'll let it pass for tonight, but you're going to have to find you someplace safer to live after that. The place isn't open for business, in the event that slipped your notice."

"No shit. Was it the broken out windows that gave you the first clue, or was it the parking lot full of grass and trees?" Saul looked in his direction, not able to see him clearly but not wanting him to know how bad it was. "Just let me out and I'll deal with things tomorrow. If all you have to do is help men who have no place to go, then you're being overpaid if you ask me."

Getting out of the cruiser was harder than he thought it should have been. His feet felt like they were asleep, and he could hardly make them work now. Allen asked him if he was all right and he flipped him off. Saul went into his hotel room, kicked off his shoes, and rubbed his feet until he was sure they were raw.

~*~

Joel looked at Miley when she came into the room. She'd graduated to a walker now, and he couldn't have been more proud of her. But as they all did, he cautioned her about doing too much too fast.

"I promise you, I'm only doing what I'm told I can do. That first day, I swear that I thought for sure that someone had pulled my legs out and replaced them with lead weights. I'm careful now." When she sat down, it was everything he could do not to help her adjust herself in the chair. She was doing better than they could have hoped for in this, and he wanted to be strong for her. "Did you know that walking will make my whole body stronger? I don't mean because I can get out more—I mean, walking helps with my heart and my lungs. The first place I'm going to go after I can walk well is into a store that didn't cater to my kind, and demand that they put in things for the handicapped. Ramps aren't that much, are they?"

"No. And from what I've read up on it, there is some kind of funding out there for it. Are you thinking of becoming an attorney?" She smiled at him, and his heart did a double beat. He loved this kid. "You'd be good at it if how you argue with me about bedtime is any indication."

"Oh, Dad." They were laughing when Mercy joined them. Just last night he'd noticed that she was showing. He'd not pointed it out to her, of course—he wasn't one that wished for death at this stage of his life. "I was telling Dad here that when I'm able to walk, I'm going to demand ramps be put in every shop."

"That's good." Miley looked at him and he shrugged. He knew that Mercy had been investigating something important, but he'd not asked about it. She was really into it last time he checked in on her. "I have a problem. Not a huge one, but enough that I'm concerned. I found out that Dante had a son. I need to find him. He's one of the others' mates."

Neither he nor Miley said anything. It was blurted out there, and he'd not had time to digest it past her having a problem. She seemed to never have anything that she couldn't work out. Before he could ask her to start over, Miley spoke.

"Is that what was in those books you're reading? By the way, those are beautiful. I'm betting it took a long time to put one of those together." Mercy told Miley it was in the books, and the books weren't hard at all if you knew what you were doing. "In class once, they showed how paper used to be made. It looked like a long process. And there are a lot of pages in your books."

"The paper vendor would have a great many screens to make them on. Plus, he'd have his family helping in drying them out, adding the right kind of herbs to make it so they'd

120

not rot." Mercy smiled at Miley. "Thank you. You got me just distracted enough that I don't feel so overwhelmed."

"This man, I'm assuming that he's an immortal like you are?" She said that he was more than likely born one. "I see. Not really, but it's not really important to the story. Why do you think he's one of the others' mates?"

"Dante wrote it in the books. It was in Latin so as not to have passersby see what it says. The queen also paid a woman by the name of Mary to watch over him. She must have been told not to tell anyone about him either. As far as I know, no one knew but the two of them." Joel asked her why it was important. "He would be our king. Even though there is no longer a castle there, he would still own the land and the stone there. It would be worth a fortune nowadays. And I looked it up—I'm still listed as the owner of it all until such time that someone of Dante's blood can claim it from me. I never understood that part. She didn't have children as far as we knew, and she died the day we were made."

"Okay. And him being mated to one of the birds, why would that matter? I'm assuming that at some point he'd have to come around, correct?" She said she didn't know, but that the mate would be queen too. "You have people out looking for him?"

"I do. I hired someone that used to search for people long ago. He has a bit of magic. People who use him, they never believe that he uses the earth to find their loved ones, but it pays well for him and he does a good job. A couple of times he's been called in to find the body or this person who has gone missing for a long time. He's really good." He asked if he was a bird. "No, he's a dragon. I was wondering if when Duncan—that's the king's name, Duncan—comes around, he'll know anything about what is in the books."

"Why does it matter? I'm sorry, did you say he's a dragon?

121

There are really dragons in the world?" Mercy said yes, there were still a few and she was still working on that. "Because you've not read all the books. That's why you're saying that."

There were dragons, his mind kept screaming at him. There were dragons around and.... His mate, she knew some. He'd have to get her to let him see one sometime. Maybe. He'd have to think on that.

"Yes, I'm only into the first book. I had been further along, but now I know to look for things in the margins and in curled pages. One of the notes I found was so close to the binding that I nearly missed it. I have to search the pages very carefully so as not to miss anything." He didn't want to sound like a doofus, so just waited for her to explain. "Why don't you ask me what you're thinking? Then I won't have to think you're thinking that I'm a doofus—whatever that is."

"I was going to ask you if you thought that I could help. Or Miley. I don't think either of us speak or read Latin, and bravo for you for knowing such an old language, but we can look if you need us to." She asked him why he thought he'd be a doofus. "Because you are so much smarter than I am, and I didn't want to have to point it out to you when it's so obvious."

"You're a nutball. And I'm not smarter than you on a great many things. I am jaded, Joel. I have been for a long time. Just having the two of you around has made all of us smarter. Thanks to the way you can think and look outside the box." He thanked her, as did Miley. "No reason for thanks. Just don't call yourself a doofus again. Whatever the hell that is."

Miley was laughing when Dutch came in to tell them that they had a guest. Not having a clue who it might be, both he and Mercy went to the door. There stood Allen, and he didn't look like this was a social visit.

They went to the living room, which was fast becoming

Joel's favorite part of the house besides the kitchen. The furniture was very comfortable, and he loved the way the plants in the room seemed to fill every corner and dark place. The air itself was cleaner smelling—fresh, he supposed. The fireplace had been lit last night to ward off the chill, and it had been amazing. A little too warm, but he could see them all there in the winter months.

"I just let your brother off at the old hotel outside of town. I have to tell you, he doesn't look good. I think he might be suffering from early onset of diabetes. That's the only thing I can think of that would be making him feel like he is." Joel told them how he'd seen him too, and Saul had told him he was fine. "He's lost a great deal of weight. And on a man his size, that's not a good thing. And he's thirsty all the time. While I was taking him from the Stop and Go, he drank down two more sodas. Something that I know for sure he shouldn't have."

"I took him food and water a few days ago. He looked scruffy then, but nothing like he does now." Allen told them that he had water out there and nothing more. "I think he's ransacked the other rooms for a bed. I noticed it the other day when I drove by and he was gone. He's set himself up nicely there."

"He's also looking for a gun. Right now I don't think he could hit the broad side of a barn, the way he's squinting all the time. That's another sign, his eye sight is going bad." Allen said that he'd keep an eye on him. "In a couple of days, if I don't see him around, I'll go and check on him. I think he'll be all right there if he won't let anyone help him. But I'll drop off some salad fixings, as well as a case or two of water. Until he's willing to go to the hospital on his own, there is little to nothing we can do about him. Now, if he gets out and does some crazy assed things, I'll have him in there so quickly that

123

he won't know what happened."

After Allen left, they sat and talked about Saul for a bit. He was for sure fighting diabetes, but how far it had gone now was anyone's guess. Like Allen had said, if he didn't want help right now, they couldn't force it on him.

"If Saul is sick, why is he acting like he doesn't have anything wrong with him? Doesn't he realize that not paying attention to something like that would make him more ill?" Miley looked down at her legs. "I was just remembering the time that I had a sore on my bottom. I couldn't feel it at all, and if you'd not found it when you did, the doctor said it could well have killed me. Why would he do that to himself?"

"Because he has always thought he was above such things, like sickness and being hurt. I remember when we were boys, he broke his arm. I don't remember how, but it was a good week before he finally admitted that it hurt. It was worse because of that. It had to be rebroken then set again." Joel thought of all the things his brother had done to him and decided never to tell his daughter. She didn't need to know the real Saul. "He'll get help with this, hopefully before it's too late. Letting something this serious go could make him have kidney problems or worse."

"If you are serious about helping me with the books, I'd appreciate the help. I can show you how to look for things in them. But the paper is very old, and some of the things are faded. Not badly, but they have been around longer than you guys have." She smiled at them both when Miley said that covered a lot of things. "Yes, I suppose it would. But tomorrow is as good a day as any. And on Saturday, we'll head over to the stash. It's in a cave that's not far from here. But only magic can open the stones there."

"Oh, how cool is that." Miley yawned as she continued, making herself comfortable on the sofa. "I'm so cozy in this room, it's my favorite place to be. Especially with my mom and dad in here with me. I think I might just take a little nap before dinner. I think that once I start walking, I'll be able to run marathons." Then she closed her eyes with a smile.

"I love her." Joel said he knew that, answering her in the same whispering voice. "I mean, I love her as much as I have anyone in my life. She's my daughter."

"Yes. And she loves you as much as you do her." Mercy nodded and left the room. Emotions were getting the better of her, he knew. Giving her time, Joel sat there and watched their daughter as she slept safely in their hearts.

Chapter 9

Allen drove his cruiser to the hotel. He could see that it was in poor shape. Perhaps when Saul was someplace else, he'd talk to the council and ask to have it torn down. That way, squatters like Saul couldn't make it their home.

When he called out for Saul, he found him in one of the many bathrooms. He was standing at the sink cutting away at the long beard he had. It looked as if he might have just started, and Allen watched him as he hacked away at the growth with a knife.

"Do you need some help?" Saul asked him if he looked like he did. "No. I was just offering. How are you feeling today?"

"Fit as a fiddle. Why do you care, anyway?" Allen didn't sit on the bed in the room. There was no telling what sort of things might be inside the mattresses. "I'll be out today. I have my eye on a few things and today is the day."

"What sort of things are those?" He didn't expect him to answer and laughed when Saul glared at him. "You need to be out of here today, Saul. I'm going to see about having this place torn down. So people like you can't just come in and make themselves at home."

"Yes, and this place is such a mansion. I'll be out, don't you worry about it." Saul put the knife down and stared at him. "You cozying up to my brother and his new wife? I hear tell she had the bucks, and stupidly gave Joel the rights to it as well. How stupid do you think she is, I wonder?"

"She's a very nice person. I like her." Saul said that he wasn't any judgement of character. "Oh? And why is that? Because I'm a cop?"

"Because you're a dumb ass. Just like Joel. Who in their right mind would turn over millions of dollars to someone like him?" Allen said people did that when they trusted. "Yes, well, I don't trust well. And what about my parents? Have you figured out if they were murdered? Not that I care one way or the other. Dead is dead, don't you think?"

"They were both murdered. And we found the axe." That got the desired reaction from Saul. He tried to look as if it meant nothing to him, but Allen could see the fear in his eyes. "It also seems that your mom had enough strychnine in her system to kill a large mammal. You wouldn't know anything about either of those things, would you?"

"I have no idea what you're talking about. And if you found the axe in the shed, then bully for you. I heard that he fell on the axe, not that he'd been hit with it." Allen hadn't said that it was in the shed but said nothing. It wasn't as if it were a confession, and certainly nothing he could use in court. "Why don't you go away? I have shit to do today, and you're keeping me from it. I told you I'd be out by today."

"Yes, well, I told Joel that I'd check on you and I have." Saul asked why Joel would even care. "I suppose because you're his brother. But since you've been a lying piece of shit all your life, I would guess that his heart, if you even have one, is bigger than yours."

128

"You're a funny cop, did you ever have anyone tell you that?" It was then that he noticed that Saul was sweating. It wasn't cold out, but it wasn't hot either. After asking him again if he was all right, the man seemed to snap. "Mother fuck, yes. How many fucking times are you going to ask me that? I answered your questions. I am leaving this shit hole today. And I am fucking all right. I want you to leave me to my business."

"You are my business, Saul."

The snort was almost comical. Allen also noticed that he was white knuckling the sink. Something was off. But right now, he didn't have a clue what it might be.

Saul did look better. He had his color back. There wasn't any kind of obvious thirst, or any of the other signs. Perhaps he'd been wrong; maybe Saul really was all right. Tipping his hat to the man, he went to his cruiser and left the lot. But not before calling Joel and letting him know what he'd found.

"If he's suffering, I honestly didn't notice it today. Perhaps it was just a case of me wanting him to be ill to get him off the streets." Joel told him not to worry about it. "You're a good man, Joel."

"Thank you. Allen, did you forget something today?" Allen said he didn't think so. "Well, I'd like for you to come on over to the courthouse and be my witness. If you remember, I asked you several days ago."

"Holy shit, I forgot. Christ, what a good friend I'm turning out to be. I'm on my way, sirens running too." He laughed as he pulled out of the parking lot. "You should hit me over the head when I get there. I'm only in my uniform."

"No worries. I'm in dress pants and a shirt. We decided that since we've already jumped the gun on a few other things, we'd just skip the being fancy." Joel was still laughing when Allen disconnected the call.

He was never late for anything. Allen showed up ten minutes early for work, never missed a day of church unless it was an emergency, and he was forever waiting for his wife to get ready at home and began telling her an hour earlier than they had to be anywhere. It had worked for a while, but she caught onto that quickly. Pulling into the parking lot, he leaped out of his car and ran, grabbing up his hat as he went. Right now, Allen could have crawled into a hole and never come out.

The courtroom was beautiful, and it had little to do with the flowers all around the room. The sisters, as everyone had been calling them, were all dressed in different shades of brown. It might have sounded drab, brown as a color, but these women made it shine. He smiled at Jude when she came to stand by him.

"She decided on having Miley as the maid of honor, which is the best that she could have done. And I'm glad you were here in time to see this." He asked her what he was seeing, because he was already blinded by the beauty. Telling him not to be such a flirt, when she nodded to his right, Allen watched Miley come into the room with just a cane to hold her up. "Miley has been working on this very hard, trying her best to be walking at her dad's wedding. They didn't know she was this far in her working with the therapist."

She had to work hard at standing upright, but she was doing it. The pride on Joel and Mercy's faces was palpable. He felt it too, all the way to his heart. Watching the little girl work this hard for her parents made him want to run home and tell his wife that he wanted seventy children right now.

He knew he couldn't do that. They had been trying for years to have a child. But after the shooting that had hit him near the groin, he no longer had the ability to father children of his own. She told him it was all right, but he felt like he'd failed her. Looking at Mercy, her small belly starting to show, he wanted to ask if for a moment he could have a bit of their magical love to help him for his wife.

But this was neither the time nor the place to be feeling sorry for himself. Allen knew that they'd someday have someone in their life, even if it was just a dog. Being a human, he knew that was about all he could hope for. Smiling, he walked to where he was to stand with Joel to be there for him. Just as the man had been there for him at times.

Joel had been around twice now when Allen was having a difficult time of something. He wasn't the captain of the station house, just a lowly cop. But there were days that he wished someone would notice. Perhaps fire the captain that they had now and give him the job and the pay. That would make it so much better for he and his wife to be able to adopt. Money and being able to afford a child were a big factor in adoption.

"I now pronounce you man and wife," Judge Wilson said to Joel and Mercy. Allen loved this couple. Allen was going to go home on his lunch hour and tell his wife just how much he loved her.

When he hugged them, and the sisters, he was pulled into a big hug again by Joel. The man, for a human, he noticed, was very huggy. Not that he minded — Allen loved a hug just as much as the next person. But when Joel whispered in his ear, Allen pulled back and asked him what he'd said.

"I have magic. A great deal of it, I'm just learning how to use some of it and other things, like dressing myself, has come fairly easy, I guess you'd say. But I do have some that I can share. So much so that I can do a lot of things that a mere human, which I am not any more, can't do. Like knowing what your greatest desire is. I would like to grant you that desire. Or I guess that I have already done it." Allen pulled away more, not sure what he was talking about and afraid that he did. "Allen, you do know that I'd never hurt you. Not in any way, shape, or form. But I wanted to help you, so I did. But I have a reason too."

"A catch, you mean?" Joel told him that it wasn't a catch, not at all, but something that he'd like for him do to. "That sounds just like a catch. And how do I know you are talking about the same thing that I want?"

"You want to give your wife a child. Children, lots of them." He nodded before he could think that he was caught in some sort of trap. "The deed, as they say, is done. You are wholly a man, though I doubt that Anna ever thought you weren't."

"She said that it didn't matter. But I hear her crying at night sometimes. Especially when she sees a family with children. Or a bump, like Mercy has." Joel sat down on one of the long pews. "What's the catch, Joel?"

"You're not going to believe me that it's not a catch, are you?" Allen sat too, his mind too busy with thinking about children. "What if I told you that I cured you of your ailment several days ago? And right now, Anna is going to have twins. I had nothing to do with that part. But you're going to have a pair of twin boys."

"I can't give her children." Joel told him that he could now, and that he had. "What is it, Joel? What is it that you need from me to make this real?"

"It is real. But what I would like for you to do, no strings, is to work with your brother. Daniel seems to think that he can work the gate twenty-four/seven, and he can't do it—not and be healthy. Not to mention, it's not necessary. But I do believe that he's having fun at the job. I want you to work when he needs a break. The house is closed up at six at night, so there is no need for either of you to be out there after that time. Magic keeps us safe then." Allen asked him about being a cop. "This is something else that I'd like for you to think about. And soon. The captain that is there now, he needs to be gone. And if you take the job that I'm offering you, someone will notice that you're doing it all. And then the ball will start rolling for you to take the position."

"I can't do both jobs." Joel told him that he'd not have to. But he could also work fewer hours for more pay. "And what about the job working with Daniel? And he does love the job. He said that you're very generous with his pay too."

"I would be with you as well. And you can continue to take over for Daniel at times. And as a captain, you'd be able to adopt children. Some that need a helping hand like you and your lovely Anna can give them." He asked about his own children. "I'm not worried about them. You shouldn't either, Allen. They'll be raised by the best and know the difference between right and wrong."

"I'd be a great father." Joel told him that he would be, yes. "I don't understand this. You're telling me that you want me to quit the force, work with Daniel, and that Anna is going to have a baby — two babies."

"Yes, and you can have more children if you wish, too. The adoption agency called Mercy for a reference. It'll be small wonder if you'll ever be turned down for anything from them." Allen smiled — he could feel it all over his body. "If I were you, I'd go home for a while, make love to your wife, write out your resignation, and start working for us today. It'll all work out, Allen, this I promise you."

Allen was nearly home when he realized that he had no idea how he'd gotten there. Nor did he remember if he'd thanked Joel or not. But he needed to see his wife, needed to know that she'd not been harmed in any way with whatever Joel had done. Allen was afraid to be hopeful on this. Terrified that it was all a dream, and he was going to wake up all the sadder for it.

When he got into the house, Anna wasn't anywhere to be seen. There were sheets out on the line—she so loved the feel of air-dried sheets. Then he saw her on the phone, talking to someone.

"Yes, I'll tell him right away, Mrs. White. He'll know just how to get the kitten out of the tree for you." She smiled at him and he walked up to her, nibbling on her neck while she talked, flustered now, to Mrs. White. "I'll do that the moment I see him. Yes, I have to go."

When she put the phone on the cradle, he turned her around and kissed her. Anna was his life, his love. Picking her up by the ass, he sat her on the counter and smiled at her.

"A little afternoon cuddling, Allen? I thought you were going to work late." He said that he'd changed his mind. "Well, Mrs. White called. If you could— Allen, you shouldn't be home making love to your wife. You should be— Oh, my yes, that's wonderful."

"I'm quitting my job and going to work with Daniel." She didn't tell him no, as he thought she would. "Joel said that he'd pay me a good wage, and that you and I are going to have a baby. Twins."

That got her attention. "I'm sorry, what?" He told her again. "That's not possible. We've seen a specialist."

"Yes, but you know as well as I that Mercy and the rest of them are magical. Just look at the things they've taken care of in town." She stared up at him, hope, a fragile thing, in her eyes. "He fixed me, he said. Several days ago. And he said that you're going to have us twin boys."

She kissed him then, wrapping her legs around his waist. Anna believed him. And as he picked her up again, heading to the bedroom, he thought that Joel might be right. He needed to quit to be what he wanted. A man with a purpose. But right now, his purpose had nothing at all to do with work, and everything to do with loving his wife.

~*~

Saul had fallen as soon as the cop left him. If he'd come back, just turned in the doorway, he might have witnessed his fall. Christ, he hurt, and was still thirsty. Leaning up on his burning legs, he put his head under the faucet and drank from it like a dog, lapping the water into his parched throat and mouth until he thought he'd explode from it.

He didn't have the strength to even go out to piss anymore. Just opening his fly, he let go of the stream of hot urine, which went all over the wall where he was kneeling. Sitting down on the floor, he half crawled and half crab walked to the bed.

There was no point in taking his shoes off and rubbing his feet anymore. His legs had joined the fight against him, making him hurt by burning up his legs with the need to massage them. Saul had figured out last night that he wasn't so much burning as he was tingling, from skin to bone, and there wasn't any way to make it stop.

If he had a gun, he'd no longer concern himself with his niece. The pain kept him up at night. He also pissed about twenty times from night to morning, then more during the day. If he had a gun, Saul would have blown his head off, the pain was that bad. Looking at the last of his food, five candy bars, he knew that he had to do something soon—even if it was only to go with the fucking cop to the doctor's office—or he was going to be found there, nothing but a shell of his former self.

To say that his pants no longer fit would have been a gross understatement. He'd taken the only sheet he could find, one that he could tear into strips, and had fashioned himself a belt. The cinch in his pants was almost twice the size as needed to cover him. And his underwear was no longer an option.

Laying there, he wondered why he was being so stupid. Not stupid, he amended to himself, but stubborn. Why not admit that he hurt? It didn't make him less of a man. And if he was better, he reasoned with himself, he could get the money that he needed to kill Miley.

"It all comes down to you getting your ass better. Don't be a moron, you moron, and get yourself help." But how? his mind screamed at him, and his body took that moment to start trembling again.

Saul had been having the shakes off and on for the last twenty-four hours. He didn't know what else could befall him, but this was the last straw. Getting down on the floor, falling on his knees and feet, Saul sat that way, sobbing about how much he ached with it all.

Crawling out of the room, he wanted to scream for help. But it would do him little to no good — there wasn't another person for miles. But almost as soon as he made his way out of the building, it started to snow, big fat flakes that rained down on his head, making him stop long enough to cry again.

Almost to the road where he thought he might be able to flag down a car, he laid there and rested. The snow was coming down heavier now, and he knew that it was going to cover him up even before anyone came by.

Saul was also afraid that if it snowed too much or started to pile up, he wouldn't ever see a car. People would be at home, basking in the heat of their nice furnaces, as well as drinking a large glass of something warm and satisfying.

"I'm going to ask for a real meal when I get someone to pick me up." He bumped his foot again and cried out. "But not before someone gives me a shot or something for this fucking pain. They'll do it, or I'll sue. That's what I'll do, sue their asses off."

Talking to himself, making himself out to be this bad assed person while he belly crawled through the rocks, mud, and snow to the road, made him feel like he wasn't less of a man. Saul had never begged for anything in his life, but right now, he'd do anything, and he did mean anything, to have some help.

His hands were raw from pulling himself along. Saul knew that his belly couldn't be in very good shape either. He wasn't anything but skin and bones. Laughing, he thought he might be lucky if he didn't break a few ribs before this was done.

The last few feet seemed to get longer with every inch he pulled himself along. The rocks were embedded in his skin around his hands. The shirt that he'd had on was nothing but rags now, and he wondered if there would be anything left of him when he was saved. It was no longer a matter of wanting to be helped, he told himself. He needed to be saved.

The car went by and splashed icy cold water into his face. For a few moments it felt wonderful. The coldness of it had made his face cooler, and the few drops that went into his mouth tasted of heaven. Just a few more feet, he kept telling himself. Just a few —

"Saul?" He knew the voice and didn't care if she was there to kill him off as she'd promised. Turning his head to look at her, he noticed that she was talking on her phone. "I'm calling for an ambulance. Don't move anymore."

He couldn't even if he had wanted to. When he heard Mercy, it was as if every muscle in his body had just said fuck it. Saul couldn't even turn to his back, to beg her for something to end the pain. Suddenly her face was too near his, and he cried out in pain when he jerked away from her.

"What the fuck were you thinking? That you'd just crawl out there to our home and try and take the money? You do know that you're suffering from diabetes, don't you?" He told her, he thought so anyway, that it was impossible. "Yes, it is. I've been reading up on it. You're a fucking moron who should have accepted help when we offered it."

"I wouldn't be taking it now if I didn't hurt so fucking bad." He heard the siren and wondered if Allen the goody cop was with them. "Just let them kill me. I've suffered enough for one man."

"Oh no. You're not getting off that easily. You're going to the hospital, getting better, and then paying for your crimes. People need closure." He started to ask her for what, but a blur of white was in his face. "Mercy, don't you dare leave me here on the side of the road. I swear to you, I will make you pay if you do."

"Side of the road? Are you serious? You're barely five feet from the hotel. You would have had to go another twenty-five to thirty feet to be there." He cried. Saul just didn't have it in him to argue with her. Besides, she was more than likely telling him the truth. "Just let these guys do their job, Saul, and I'll call Joel."

"I don't want him to see me like this." Mercy told him too bad and walked out of his vision. The pinch of something at his arm made him turn to the men leaning over him, and then he started to fuzz out. But he wasn't done with Mercy. Yelling for her, he saw her just as he was being lifted up to be in the back of the ambulance. He was indeed only a few feet from the hotel, and too far from the road. He would never have made it, Saul realized now.

Letting the fuzz, whatever it was, take him under, Saul heard one of the men say something about his foot and leg. He couldn't quite make it out, but it sounded to him like they were saying that he might need to have it broken in three places. That couldn't be right. But he was too far gone with the meds they gave him to care what they did to him. But no one had better be breaking his leg. He needed to get Miley and kill her for Joel to come to heel again.

Chapter 10

Mercy was waiting in the waiting room for Joel when he showed up. Saul had bypassed the emergency room and had been taken right to surgery. The doctor didn't hold out much hope for the man. He had let things get too bad for too long.

After Mercy told him everything she'd found when she'd gotten there and what she'd learned from the doctor, he sat down on one of the chairs in the room. Mercy also told Joel that he might lose not just his leg, but a part of his foot on the other leg as well.

"I hadn't any idea that it had gotten that bad, did you?" She shook her head and sat down next to him. "When Allen told me earlier that he thought Saul might be getting better, I didn't even think to come and check on him. And had you not been going for pizzas for us, he might well have died out there."

"You can't blame yourself for this, Joel. He had plenty of opportunities to get himself help. Even Allen said he told him that he was a diabetic. Saul was stubborn, and this is all on him." She thought about the things that Saul had said in the ambulance drive over, and nearly didn't tell Joel. But

141

they were not going to keep secrets from each other, they had promised that. "He said that they'd better not take off his legs. He said that he was going to need them to kill our daughter. Something about it bringing you to heel. Again. He said that he'd have to kill her to bring you to heel again. What happened?"

"We had a dog. Or I had a dog. His name was Snow. He was white, too, all over his body, except for the very tip of his tail. Mom suggested that I call him Tippy, but that just seemed so obvious. So, he was Snow." When he leaned back, taking her hand to his heart, she wasn't sure she wanted to hear anymore. Saul was a bastard, and there was no telling what sort of evil things he'd done to that poor dog. "One afternoon, just after my birthday, the mail ran. I got a card from my grandma with two ten-dollar bills in it—a fortune to a ten-year-old. I gave Mom one of them, so she could buy the stuff to make me a cake, and she said that there would be money left over—what else did I want? I told her to get a box of chocolates, big enough to share with the entire family. That was a treat that we all enjoyed, especially my father."

The nursing staff was quiet on this floor, and they were moving back and forth between rooms helping the patients. Once a light went on for a room, they wasted no time in going there and figuring out what was wrong. Mercy had been a doctor once, not long ago, and she had treated her nursing staff with courtesy, as well as humor. They would get very little of that from anyone else they worked with, she had noticed. Joel started talking again, and she turned her attention back to him.

"Snow would meet me at the bus every day. The other kids were excited to see her as much as I was. She'd try to get on the bus with me too, I guess to help me off faster, and that would delight them as well. But of course, Saul hated her.

142

Mom was going to pick up something for Snow to celebrate my birthday with me." She held his hand tighter when he seemed to be upset a little. "Mom left me there with Saul. And the entire time she was gone, he wanted me to give him the other ten. I was going to take us to the movies, just he and I, but he wanted it all. Anyway, while our parents were gone, he and I got into a fist fight. Well, he beat the crap out of me, and I laid there and took it. Usually I just passed out from it, and this time was no different. Not a long time, but enough that he'd get bored waiting on me to wake up and would leave me alone."

"I bet he was a bully at school too, wasn't he?" Joel told her that he was at home, suspended, more than he was attending class. "Yes, I can see that about him. He just gives off an aura of meanness."

"As soon as Mom pulled our Chevy Rambler into the driveway, I knew that something had happened. She stood out by the car for so long that I didn't want to go out. But she looked at me while I watched her and started crying." Joel told her that he'd been hiding behind the couch, waiting on their mom to come home and save him. "I finally went out. I told myself I was ten and there wasn't anything to be afraid of anymore. But I saw Snow as soon as I got to Mom."

Tears fell down Joel's cheeks. She didn't want him to remember any more, but she knew that it would be next to impossible for him not to finish the story. He needed to tell her more than she needed to hear it.

"He'd taken a knife to her. Cut her head off and left it there so they'd know what they were looking at. But that wasn't enough for Saul. It was never enough if he could do more. He'd taken the lawn mower and had run over Snow's little body over and over until there was nothing left of her but scraps of fur and blood." Joel held her to his chest as he continued. "If that wasn't bad enough, he knocked the chocolate cake that my mom had gotten on clearance, because it was more festive than she could have made, to the ground. Smashing it with his bare feet, he made sure that there wasn't a bit of it left for anyone to eat.

"He taunted me later, as he was stood in the corner after Dad had beaten his ass. Saul told me whenever we were alone in the kitchen that the next time he told me to do something, I'd better do it. Laughingly, he also told me how he'd found the money that I'd hidden away and had burned it. I believed him. There were remnants of it still in the kitchen near the stove." Joel looked exhausted after that, but he told her the rest. "After that, I would just simply give the money to my mom when I had any. Stashing it away never did me any good with Saul around. Then when he was fifteen, he hit my mom and they sent him away for five years. That was the first stint of prison for Saul. But far from the last."

They sat there in silence for the most part, only talking when people came by to see how they were doing. The man who ran the deli in the hospital, a person that one of her sisters had helped out, brought them thick sandwiches. While she told Joel she wasn't hungry either, he reminded her that she was going to have a baby and needed to eat. They both ate half of one of the big subs before they'd had more than enough.

The nurse came out to give them updates every hour or so. It was going on five hours now since Saul had entered surgery, and it looked like it might be a few more before they were finished. The other birds came to sit with them. and someone had even brought Miley.

"This is a hell of a wedding night." She laughed with Joel. "I'll make it up to you soon. After all this is over. Right now, I want to just make sure that Saul isn't going to be any trouble and that he's all right. I don't know why I care, but I do."

"Because he wouldn't." She looked hard at Esme when she spoke. "Don't give me that look. You know as well as we all do that had that been Joel on the side of the road, he could have more than likely laughed at him as he laid there dying. Not lifting a finger to help at all."

"You're right. He is a bastard." Joel stood up with the rest of them when the doctor came down the hall. He was still in scrubs and his face looked exhausted, but he smiled when he told them all to have a seat. "What did you have to do, Doctor?"

Doctor Brian Wayne had been a friend of theirs for some time now, since Remi had recruited him to come to their little town and work there. Since then he'd set up a practice with his wife, become the go to man at the hospital, as well as become a member of the school board with Joel. He was a good man.

"I have to tell you, it was touch and go there for a while. He's lost a great deal of weight, and it's taken its toll on his heart and other organs. We did have to remove his left leg to the thigh. He'd let it go too long. And since he wasn't eating right nor taking any care of the wound, the blood poison ran throughout his system quickly. I'm sorry, but we may yet have to remove this right foot too." Mercy asked about his hands — they were bad when she'd seen them. "Yes, they were. After cleaning the gravel and other dirt out, it was determined that we'd leave them for now. He was in the worst shape that I've seen for a while. And Mr. Oliver, he's been a type two diabetic for what I would say is most of his life. He was just lucky, until the end here, that it didn't get the better of him sooner."

"Should I be tested for it as well? And I have a daughter too. Should we be worried?" The doctor explained that if they hadn't had trouble with it before now, they were probably fine. But to keep an eye on it, and that testing wasn't a bad idea. "Yes, we will."

The doctor explained that they'd have to be gowned up to go and see Saul for the next several days. If there was a chance of infection or if they had anything like a cold, then he'd prefer that they didn't visit.

"He's going to need long-term care after this. I'm not sure what his situation is, but he isn't going to be able to be left on his own for a while. If ever. He's going to be confined to a wheelchair for sure, and unless he comes to terms with what's happened to him and what he needs to do to be healthy, then I'm afraid the prognosis isn't going to be good for him." No one said that they'd make sure he did. The doctor noticed it too. "I'm assuming that he's not on the best of terms with any of you. He gave my people a hard time, mentioning that he needed a gun to kill someone named Miley."

"That would be our daughter." Joel looked at his daughter, then back at the doctor. "No, we're not on the best of terms with him, but we'll make sure that he has care. My wife and I will talk it over, and we'll get back with you on what we can do."

"Whatever it takes." Joel kissed her when she chimed in. "We will do whatever it takes to make him comfortable and safe. But we can't let him in our home. Not ever. He's been trying to kill Miley since he showed up at our door, almost as soon as he was in town."

"I understand. I've heard about him, living out there in the hotel all alone. I have to tell you, I thought that perhaps it was something like that. I know you well enough, Mercy, that I know that you'd not deliberately leave someone to die like that." She thanked him. "No need for that. But I will warn you, he'll need care, a great deal of it, as I said. If you'd like, I can make arrangements to have him set up in a long-term care nursing home that will help him cope. I think, knowing

146

him as I have the last few hours, he'd need that so that he'll follow the rules in keeping him on a diet plan."

"Yes, all right. You set that up and we'll make arrangements to pay the bills too." Brian nodded at Mercy, then left them there to see that things were set up immediately. Joel looked at her when the doctor left them. "Are you all right with this? I mean, he'll be close, but I'm thinking he won't be coming to the house anytime soon."

"Yes, I'm very all right with what you've done for him. All I've ever wanted to do since we were children is shove him in a hole someplace and forget him. But since meeting you, I've come to the decision that no matter what he tries to do to us, he's still family." Mercy said that was correct. "Thank you. Thank you all for standing with me on this. I just don't know what I'd do if you weren't a part of my life."

Dinner was a pizza. The subs that they'd had earlier hadn't hit the spot, and now they were all starving. It wasn't as if the subs weren't good—they were very good. But they had been stressed out, and now they needed to celebrate. Not because Saul was still ill, but because for now anyway, he was going to be all right. And safe. Mercy was glad for that. She wasn't sure that Joel could have stood for his brother dying the way he might have out there alone.

~*~

Joel sat near the bed that Saul was lying in. He was still in the hospital after ten days, and Joel had come by a couple of times a day to check up on him. The second surgery had really ended all chances of Saul living a normal life. His right foot had had to be removed the second time in the operating room, as well as part of one of his fingers on his right hand. The dirt in a hangnail had gotten so infected that they feared for his life.

The day before yesterday he'd sat down with Mercy, and

147

they worked out a plan with the doctor. The nursing home for Saul was set up now, as well as an exercise program to keep him in shape. He also had a very strict diet that he was going to be on, and a pump to regulate his insulin for the rest of his life. Saul was not going to be happy about any of this.

Joel looked at his brother. Saul had awakened several times when he'd been there. Mostly he'd just stare at him, never saying a word, then close his eyes and turn so that the back of his head was facing him. Joel had learned not to say anything to him. He was sure that this was just another one of those times until Saul spoke to him.

"Where am I?" Joel told him. "You left me out there to die, didn't you? You poisoned my food and made me ill."

"No. Whatever happened to you, you did that all on your own." Saul closed his eyes again and didn't say another word. Joel got up and stretched—it was time that he left anyway. He was working a good job and having a blast at it.

Miley was still here working on strengthening her legs, so he stopped by to see if he could take her home. She was all for it, especially since he was taking her to lunch. As soon as she was finished up and had her shower, they were headed out of the hospital.

"Saul asked me again where he was. Then he accused me of leaving him out there to die. If I didn't already have a dislike of the man, I would now, the way he keeps repeating himself." Miley was walking well now. She still had a cane for her balance, which she was still getting used to. But he did help her into the car. He sat there on his knees after lifting her legs in and told her he was sorry.

"For what?" Joel told her. "Dad, I know that you don't like him. I don't either, for all the things that he was planning to do to me. That, I have to tell you, was a real eye opener. He laid out all the paper at the hotel to wrap me in, even putting my name on the sheets. But even before that, he wasn't very nice to us. I remember him coming by the house. The things he said to you."

"I love you, Miley. And I'm so very proud of you." She kissed him on the forehead and told him to stop being sappy and feed her. "I can always depend on you to put me where I belong. All right, my dear, what's it to be? Pizza, burgers, or would you like a sub?"

"I want to go to that pizza place that Remi is starting up. It looked good when I spell checked her menu." She'd been helping all of them out a great deal lately, and even though she'd not wanted any money for it, she was getting a nice sized bank account for herself.

The place was busy, but mostly due to the staff being trained. There were two people for every table waiting on folks, and it was a little overwhelming. But Remi had decided to have too many at first—most were not cut out for food service, she thought—rather than to not have enough when it was time for the grand opening. If the soft opening—without advertising that they were there yet—was any indication, she was going to have a hit on her hands.

They enjoyed the pizza as well as the iced tea. Mercy didn't drink coffee or any sodas, so he'd gotten used to drinking what she did. Miley drank milk—a great deal of it, as a matter of fact. Remi came out to sit with them and brought out a platter of different foods for them to try.

"Those are going to be twist ups. I'm going with a fifties sort of theme in here. I know there's and old jukebox in storage that I'm going to bring here too." They tried all the different flavors and gave all but one the okay. "Yeah, wasn't sure about that one. I know there are a lot of people who like black olives, me included, but they're not to everyone's taste. Mercy said that we're going out to the stash today. I haven't

149

any idea why we still call it that. It's a frigging cave. Anyway. I have a few ideas that I'd like to bring back with us. I bought a house. Did I tell you?"

"Yes, Mercy mentioned it. She said that it's really old and that it needs some work done on it." Miley asked her if she was going to do all the work herself.

"No way. I have better things to do with my time than to put in plumbing again." Miley asked if she'd done that before. "I think that we've all done just about everything at one point in our lives. Mercy and I were doctors together. It wasn't my cup of tea, so to speak. I wanted to heal them all, but I realized that it wouldn't go over well. Mercy just didn't like it from the start, but she stuck with it longer than I did. I think she might still have her license. I remember that Esme was a pirate. She really enjoyed that." That got Miley excited. Remi told her of all the things that she'd done that she could remember. It had been a long time.

When they were getting ready to leave, Mercy joined them. She had been scoping out a couple of places to put in a grocery store. The one that they had had in the town had burnt to the ground about five years ago. The need for one was great, as it took almost forty minutes to drive to the one in the next town over.

"I have two places that I think will work. And some of the pack have said that they'd help with the construction. That will be helpful all the way around. Income and a place to buy milk." She took one of the twisters off the plate and spit it out on her napkin. "That is gross. Who would want black olives in their bread?"

Joel was still laughing as they left the restaurant. His cell was ringing as he was walking to his car, and he knew it was the hospital. Answering it, he was asked to come back to see his brother, as he was asking for him.

"He's done this before. Is he awake enough to know that he's asking for me?" The nurse assured him that he was indeed awake, and that they'd had to restrain him. "I'm sorry. I'll be right there."

They decided to go with him, Miley and Mercy. They were riding up in the elevator to his floor when Mercy asked Miley if she'd like to wait with her, give Joel time with his brother. She looked so relieved that he was glad that Mercy had suggested it. But he wasn't looking forward to seeing his brother on his own.

Saul was yelling when he entered the room. The nurse was trying her best to put Saul at ease, but he wasn't having any of it. He was telling her to shut the fuck up and to get his brother. Joel knew that he could do this, talk to Saul, because he was stronger than he'd ever been before.

Putting both his fingers in his mouth, Joel let out a whistle that even impressed him. But the room grew suddenly silent, which was what he wanted.

"Where the hell have you been? I've been calling out for you for an hour." Joel simply sat down and asked the nurse to leave them alone. She ran out of the room like she'd been reprieved from prison. "Answer me, you fucking bastard. Where have you been?"

"Having a nice lunch with my wife and daughter. And I was here not an hour ago and you were still out. We have to talk, Saul. There are things you need to be made aware of." Saul asked him when he was getting out of here. "You're not. Not for a while, anyway. You've had some major surgery, and you're still healing."

Saul looked down at his hand but said nothing about the thick bandage around it, smeared in blood. Joel decided to wait on him to ask. It wasn't going to change things for him to blurt it all out at one time.

"That wife of yours, she brought me here under duress. I'm going to sue her for everything that she has for doing that." Joel waited for him to get whatever it was out of his system. "Well, jackass? Are you going to tell me what happened to my hand?"

"They had to remove one of your fingers." Saul paled but said nothing. Joel leaned back in his chair as he continued. "It was infected from the hangnail that you had there. If you'd gotten help sooner, when it was offered to you, you might have been in better shape all the way around."

Saul glanced at his legs but turned away. There was a tent-like thing over his lower half. It looked like his legs were having a strange and peculiar campout. Saul asked him where his wife was.

"In the waiting room with Miley. The police found the newspapers that you laid out to put her in when you murdered her. Why did you do that, put her name on each sheet?" Saul laughed, telling him so Joel would know it was from him. "Yes, well, that's a moot point now, isn't it?"

"You think so? I'm still going to hurt you, Joel. In a way that you're never going to recover from it. I'm going to kill that daughter of yours and do just want I said, lay her in that open pit so that the rodents can get to her pretty face." Joel felt his bird run along his skin. If Saul felt it, the magic, he didn't mention it. "Then I'm going to take what I can from you before I kill off you and that wife of yours. Why she gave you all the money too is beyond me. But it will go a long way in making up for you making it so I lost my finger."

"You lost your leg too. And your foot on the other leg. You're lucky that you didn't lose them both to the thigh. How much will that cost for you to pay me back?" It was cruel, and he hated himself for saying it like that, but his brother was hurting him too. "Would you like to see?"

152

Instead of waiting for him to answer, Joel stood up and jerked the tent off his bed. There was blood on the little blue padding on the bed, and the stumps where his foot and leg had been were bleeding through. Saul just stared at them, like he was trying to take it all in.

"You did this to me." Joel wanted to point out that he'd done nothing to him at all. "You left me out there to die, and when you had the chance, you had them operate on me so that I'd be a cripple all my life."

"You did this to yourself, Saul. You knew that you were a diabetic. They told you about it ten years ago. The prison knew it, and that's why you were on a diet there. They said that they even gave you a prescription to get filled to make sure you were okay. But you never once picked it up. Why? Why would you do that to yourself?" Saul pulled his eyes away from his body to glare at him. "You can be upset with me all you want, but we both know this was all your doing."

"You think you know everything, don't you? A man with a wife, money to burn, and you have not one thing to give to me. All your life you got whatever you wanted, while I was left in the dust. Mom even made you cakes for your birthday. All I got was a single cookie." He asked him if Mom had known what his health was like. "Of course she did, you moron. That's why she hated me so much. I had to have everything special to eat. But I wanted everything to be special for me all the time, like new clothing when you didn't get some, a new coat instead of the used one that Dad had outgrown, I never got anything because Mom and Dad hated me."

"Because we were broke, Saul. Didn't you understand that?" Saul asked him why that should matter to him. "Because to give you everything that you wanted, we would have had to go without. Don't you see that?"

"Again, how is that my burden to carry? I'm special. And

153

everyone needs to see that." Joel sat back down after laying the cover over Saul. "Like that's going to make it any better, you fucking idiot. You had them take me apart so that you think you'll be safe from me. But you won't be. Not ever. I want you to go out, kill someone, and bring their legs to me. The doctor will just have to put them back on me."

"You can't be serious." Saul asked him why he thought that he wasn't. "Because first of all, I'm not killing anyone for you. Ever. And secondly, there isn't any way that anyone is going to put you back together. This is what you did to yourself by not taking care of your body."

Joel stood up.

"Sit your ass back down. I'm far from finished with you." Joel started to sit — it had been ingrained into his head to obey Saul or face the pain. But he stood his ground, lifting his chin up, feeling like a better man. "You sit that fucking ass of yours down and do what I told you. I will not be a cripple, Joel. I'm not a man that can deal with that sort of thing. Do what I told you, now."

"No." Joel felt better for that, standing up to Saul and standing his ground. "No, I will not be your whipping boy again. You've been set up to go to a nursing home after here. They'll make sure that you're on a diet that won't kill you off. And they'll help you acclimate yourself to being unable to walk. After that, I believe you'll go back to prison, one that can care for your needs. I hope you have a good life, though if I was honest with you, I could care less if you do or not. I'm going to tell the desk not to contact me anymore. I won't come here again; none of my family will visit you. And you'll be all alone. The way you should have been all along."

Joel left Saul then. After stopping by the desk and telling them what he wanted, he made his way to his family. Hugging them to him, Joel could hear Saul down the hall, still

154

screaming for him to come back and kill someone for him. And to pay him.

"Let's go home, all right?" They did, talking about anything but Saul on the way there. "After we get the truck to go to the storage unit, I'd very much like to have dinner and make plans to go on a long trip with my favorite girls. Then, when we return, we'll set up the nursery."

"Sounds like a wonderful plan." Mercy kissed him and held him before they went into the house. "Are you all right?"

"Yes. I think I am. I'm not going to see him again. I can't do that. It's too much." Mercy said she understood. "Thank you. For everything. I love you."

"And I love you."

Chapter 11

The storage warehouse that they'd used over the decades needed some repairs. Mercy was just looking at one of the smaller pieces when she spied a cracked window. Yes, she decided, it was time to get this thing updated. Perhaps even put in a bathroom or two. She was forever having to pee nowadays.

They found the jukebox right away, even plugged it in and listened to the old tunes on it as they searched for anything they wanted. It had been a long time since anyone had been in here, and there was a memory with everything they uncovered. She found the canopy bed just as she was thinking about it. Miley squealed with delight when Piper, who had owned it, said she could have it.

"But what about if you have a daughter? Won't you want her to have it?" Piper laughed and uncovered the second one. "You have two of the same bed? What on earth for?"

"I forgot that I had it. You have to remember, we have been around for a long time. That one that I gave you was in the castle when we raided it. Dante, I think, would have loved for you—the first of many grandchildren, I'm betting—

to have it. It's all hand made. But I do think you'll need to have a mattress special made for it. It's very wide and long."

There was a dresser that went with it, and a high boy. Things for Miley were set, as far as the little girl was concerned. Mercy was still looking for the queen's bed when Joel unearthed a large trunk.

"Do you have the key to it?" Mercy told him to touch it, saying special words. "Seriously? That's all I have to do?"

"Yes, keys were basically the same back then and forever coming up missing. So Dante came up with a way for it to work without one." Joel asked her what the words were. "*Falcon, hawk, eagle, phoenix, vulture,* and *owl.* Us."

"Why not your names?" Esme said that they didn't have names back then. They had picked out their own. "So, you thought of Mercy?"

"Yes, well, there's a gory story that goes with that." Mercy looked at Blaze when she said she wanted to tell it. "It's not true, just so you know."

"It is true. She would forever be begged for mercy while we were fighting. One man begged her for mercy over and over until it sort of stuck with her. So, whenever anyone saw her great falcon coming for them, they'd start begging. Mercy wasn't much given back in those days, so you know."

The trunk was opened, and Mercy watched as Miley and Joel took out several of the pieces and marveled over them. Some of the pieces of jewelry she remembered, but most she didn't. There were bejeweled knives, as well as a couple of crowns that they'd won in victory. Also, some very pretty gems, none of which had meant anything to them at the time.

"I'd like to take one of these and put it in my room. If that's all right with you guys." They all agreed that Miley could have it. "I know that it's expensive and I will take care of it. But I'd like to wear it sometimes. Just to feel like a queen."

"Well, that one is a male crown." They all laughed when Miley put it back in the trunk. But Piper bent and picked up a smaller one, one that was much more ornate than the rest. "This one, I believe, was taken from a woman that had stolen it from the castle we were raiding. She had tried to buy me off with it. Of course, like Mercy, we didn't take it. What use would a giant bird have with a crown anyway?"

Miley still wanted it, even after the story. It was beautiful with all the gold and gems.

As Mercy made her way through the rest of the things in the warehouse, she looked around for some of the furniture that they'd wanted for the new house.

"There is a bed over there that is the biggest bed I've ever seen." She followed Joel to where it was broken down and leaning against the wall. "I mean, from the width of the headboard, I'd say it's about eight feet wide. What the hell kind of mattress would that take?"

"Not a mattress back then. Ticking. And straw. If someone was very wealthy, they'd have wool in it. But that usually would bring out all kinds of critters." She didn't know where it had come from, however. "We would take things from the castles that we destroyed to sell, or to be used by someone that needed things. Mostly the wooden things, like this, would have been split up and used for fire. I don't have any idea why this was saved. But I do know that these marks here? They're from Esme's claws when she carried it back to the encampment. If you want it, which I don't mind at all, we can have a mattress made for it."

"I do. I don't know why. It's very ornate and dark, but I love the dragons on the posts, as well as the one curled up at the top of the headboard. It'll be like we're being watched over as we sleep." Joel grinned at her as he continued. "I've been meaning to ask you, were there dragons during your

159

time?"

"There were. Not as many as there used to be before we started wars, but there were enough to darken the skies during the day. Their flames were hot enough to burn down a village as they flew by. And when sheep came up missing, it was said that they'd taken them, when more than likely the few that were gone had been taken by a neighbor or a passing family." He shivered, and she smiled. "Did you think that there wouldn't be? I mean, look at the detail on the dragon there. Where do you think that design stemmed from?"

"I was hoping, I guess, that someone had a great imagination. I know you mentioned it before, but I didn't let my mind wrap around it. I guess I was hoping you were teasing me." She told him not for that. "Yes, well, I can see that now. What else have you found? I have to admit, I love that table. It's sort of barbaric looking with the chairs like they are, but it appeals to me on a certain level."

It was a long thinnish table that would seat fourteen, if the chairs were any indication. She had kept it from one of the last castles that they'd invaded. Like Joel, she had no idea why it appealed to her, or even what she thought she'd do with it as a bird. But it might have been the way the table looked just like what it was—a large middle slice of a grand old tree.

The chairs were barbaric in how they were adorned. Atop each of the ears, the very tip of the back rails, was an animal of the forest. Rabbits and moles. There were birds too, smaller ones like the others might have been. But the head chair, it had a tall falcon on each side, and the arms were carved to look like the wings.

She'd only just realized that she'd never sat in the thing. For all she knew it could be the most uncomfortable dining set she'd ever seen. Joel sat down in it and smiled. She waited for him to tell her that he hated it, but instead, he told her that it was comfortable. Like a man twice or so his size had made it soft and pliable for him to use. Mercy sat down in one of the other chairs and felt the same thing. Like it had been made for them to use.

"There is a great deal of stuff in here." She told Jude that she'd forgotten how much. "I was at first thinking that we could sell it off — we don't really have much use for this much furniture — but then I had a better idea. I think I'm going to buy the Darkberry Mansion and turn it into a bed and breakfast. I think that sucker has like fifteen bedrooms."

"You'd use this stuff in it?" Jude nodded and said that whatever they didn't want, or she didn't want to keep, they could put a price tag on it at the B&B. "That's wonderful, Jude. I mean, with the restructure of the town and businesses coming in, it would be sort of neat to have something like that for people to stay in. Also, Blaze is talking about putting some of the smaller pieces and the pictures that we have into a museum-like setting that people might want to see as well. I think there are some plates and things over in one of the other trunks that you can use. And a lot of stuff in the cave."

"Cave? I thought this was it. I mean, you said cave before, but this is dark and such. I just assumed this was all there was." Jude told Joel this wasn't even a drop in the hat of what they had stored away. "More furniture too?"

"No, the cave would have been damp after all these years, so at some point in all this time we commissioned to have this place built. Mostly it was used for crops and such, but that soon died out. But this stuff, it's been in here for centuries. We had fans put in some time ago, then later there was a dehumidifier installed. It's why everything is so dry and without mold. We're going there today. You should see what you can have there too."

161

The trip was planned, but Miley wasn't going this time. They were headed there as birds, and she wasn't able to fly just yet. She could be a bird, they'd found out, but she was still having balance issues, and so she had to wait before taking to the air.

It didn't take long to get there, but the flight was made longer by all of them playing in the sky. It had been a long time since they'd all had been together like this. And having Joel there to see his enjoyment through fresh eyes made them all happy. The trees were just turning too, their colors so bright in the evening sun that Mercy wanted to linger longer, just to be free of the stress of life right now. Landing near the opening, she put her hand on the large stone and said the words that would open it. Nothing so fancy as the names of their birds. It was simply "Lady Dante, Queen of Castle Duncan, give me entrance."

The large stone groaned as it moved out of its resting place. There had been weeds and trees growing around the area, and instead of killing them with the stone moving, they simply moved out of the way. Dante wanted nothing or no one to suffer unnecessarily.

The entrance was bright with sunlight. Mercy knew that the deeper they went into the belly of the mountain it would grow darker. As soon as they reached the cave where they had stored things—the queen had saved all this for them—the way would be bright again. The mountain, knowing who they were, would open an opening wide and deep so that the sunlight would be surrounding them in the place of treasures.

"Oh my. Oh my, oh my. There is much more than I could even imagine here." Joel walked around the trunks and piles of coins and gold. Silver too was stashed in here, as well as gems the size of his head. "You could put the national banks out of business with all this."

He never touched anything, Mercy noticed, but kept his hands at his back while he peeked into whatever he saw that interested him. Leaving him to look around, she went to the walls to find what she'd wanted since falling in love with the man.

The rings were just where she'd seen them last — wedding bands made of the purest silver and adorned with a single diamond on the woman's band. The diamond was pink, a lovely shade of the palest color she'd ever seen. She knew, too, where she'd gotten it from. Joel joined her when she called for him.

"The ship that was bringing the king to Dante's castle had these on his ship when he was coming across the sea. There were many more pieces he brought — not for Dante, but for the new bride that was being held in the lower chambers of the ship." Joel took both pieces and asked her what happened to the woman. "She was nearly dead when we got to the boat. They had forgotten about her, I guess, and she starved, too weak to try and move. It wouldn't have mattered to him, I don't suppose — it had not mattered to him that she didn't want to come with him. She had a husband of her own, four sons too. I guess that is why he took her — she was ripe to bear him a son."

"You killed him." She nodded, then shook her head. "I'm assuming that you all did. Went out to sea to kill the man who took your queen's life, so to speak?"

"No, it was only I that sunk the ship. I was angry, you see. Not because Dante had died, but that she had given us the ability to shift into humans. The others were happy, in a way, I guess. I blamed it all on him. It was, I guess, his fault really. But to me, he was the sole reason that she had died. So, I took the biggest boulder I could find and dropped it from a great height to sink his ship. But I promise you, Joel, I saved anyone that was there against their will. And there were quite a few of them."

"And these rings? You found them while searching the ship?" She told him that she'd found them when she'd found the bride. They were hers and her husband's. The king had killed her family so that she'd be free to go. "Such a sad story to go with a set of wedding rings. Don't you think?"

"Perhaps. But you see, she begged me to take them with me before she died. To give them love and life again. That the sorrow that was attached to them should be erased by a true love, one that could make the wrong right for her. She told me to marry someday, have many children, and give the rings to my first-born son, that he too could find happiness in such a beautiful beginning."

"That's very lovely." He slipped her ring on her finger and she did the same to his. The rings fit them as if they'd been made only for them. "I will give you as much happiness and safety as you have given me and mine. I will only love you, Mercy Oliver, for the rest of my days."

They kissed, and it felt like they were married for the first time.

~*~

Duncan watched them as they moved in and out of the cave. He'd been waiting here for so long that he despaired of them ever coming. When he saw the younger man with them, he smiled. Mercy had found her mate.

He knew who was going to be mated to whom. His mother had left him a thick book of things that she'd seen in the future. She'd also told him about his own mate, and how she would make him happy.

"She will make you the king that I know you will become. The lands, all that I ever had, they are for you, waiting. Mercy will gladly turn them over to you. But do not allow her to think herself less than you. She will, because she is a good person. Her mate, he will make her feel things that she never felt when she was my bird."

Duncan had seen the birds, of course. He had lived in the castle proper his entire life, as well as when the encampment had been moved for safety reasons. His mother had even known that Mercy would end the life of the king. It would be written that he was killed at sea from a great storm. So far, all her tales and stories had been right. But the mate for him, Mother had said she was pretty. Duncan thought her to be a vision.

Her name and what she did was lost to him. He thought perhaps it was because she was related to him, in a way. His other, she'd told him only that she was a bird and one of her six. Over the years he'd been able to narrow it down to which one, just not her name. Duncan had determined which one she was by knowing what the others were. Their names were difficult to get, but he was getting them.

Approaching Mercy would have to wait for a while longer. There was trouble coming, as there usually was around him, that would make Blaze a target of great wrath. And she would be harmed, as would her own mate. But it was his mate that he worried for. She too, he thought, would be injured.

Joel was trying to keep his load to a minimum. But the others, the other birds, were putting more into his pack than he would carry. The man did not know yet that he could carry much more than a human could, and would still be able to fly high, even as a small bird. He looked at the opening of the cave when a glint of something flashed over his eyes.

The sword of Duncan Castle. It had hung over the fireplace, he'd been told. Duncan had seen his mother from time to time. She would visit him when she made her rounds, and they'd talk about the way life was going to be for him and his Mary. Most of the time she would bring him food, some sweet treat. But as he grew older, she brought him books to read. Numbers to look over, as well as a great many other things.

Duncan could read and speak any language. His ability to work on a computer was known worldwide. He could also fight with a sword, gun, or even his fists as any great fighter of any time. His mother had made sure that he was a learned man. One that could have a conversation with his mate, or anyone for that matter, and not seem out of place.

When they were finished with their work, he waited until they took to the skies before he entered the cave as well. There were things that they'd taken that he was glad for, but now he had to leave behind the books.

Soon he'd talk to Mercy, and she'd have to come and get them to read. But for now, they were where she could find them—and he knew that she would. Mercy had his mother's books now and was reading them over for information. Duncan wondered if she'd figured out that he had been born. More than likely, he thought. Mercy was the smartest of all the birds.

Putting the books near the opening, he walked around, not really seeing the things that he'd seen hundreds of times before. But he did find one thing that he thought to take with him this time. The ruby that was as big as his fist. It would be for his mate, his bride.

There were times when he needed to come here, to make it so he had coin, but of late it hadn't been necessary. All the people that he was still caring for as king, he paid out of his own earnings. Money for them wasn't that much, but he had made a promise and he would hold to it. Besides, there were only a few left, four at last counting.

Mary was like him, an immortal, and she would remain

with him even after he took his mate. She was to be his cook first, then nanny to his children. She would teach them all the ways of a child of royalty, and he would love them with his wife as much as he could.

There was Jacob as well. He had been a maker of swords when he'd been younger. He still looked to be only in his mid-twenties, a skilled man well beyond the years he looked. The money that he made, it went back into his work. Jacob made decorative swords for people around the world. None of them, he promised, would ever be used to take a life. It was the magic that he put into each of them that made it so.

Cowell was also in his home. He served as his butler and best friend. They had grown up together, him being Mary's only son. No matter how many times he begged the man to go out on his own, to be the rich man that he was, he felt that his place was with Duncan, and he would stay until Duncan's children's children had children. Smiling, he thought that to be a very long time indeed.

Leaving the cave the way he'd found it, Duncan leaned against the stone and could almost feel the warmth of his mother there. She'd not been like most of the queens he'd heard about in books, nor the ones that he'd encountered long after his mother was gone. Mom wasn't cold like they seemed to be. Nor did she turn away from a hug. Mary told him that she had changed his dirty nappy and fed him when he was slinging his mush around the room.

It was her laughter that he could remember more than anything. Her face had faded away over time. Her soft hands he could no longer see. But her laughter and the smell of her skin, that would come to him forever.

Fresh linens. That was what she smelled like, with just a touch or rosemary for scent. Whenever he smelled that today, cooking or just growing in the gardens as it did around his estate, he thought of his mother.

Her laughter wasn't soft like her skin, however. She brayed like a donkey. Great gulping gasps of air as she exhaled the most horrific sound. But she cared not what she sounded like, he began to think. For she laughed often and loudly. All the time.

Duncan made his way back to the area where he'd landed. He hadn't taken flight as Mom's birds had. He couldn't fly, not yet. He had to wait for his mate, and she'd be with him soon enough. The small helicopter took off without a sound other than the swish-swish of the blades as they cut through the air.

Mary was waiting for him as he came to the front of the house. She would pepper him with questions, all of which she'd know the answer to, and he'd send her to the kitchen for either a cup of her tea or a glass of the same amber liquid. It was one of his true loves of food, tea.

"The invitations have gone out." He turned and looked at Mary, asking her what she was talking about. "To the Christmas party that you said you'd host."

"Yes, I remember. All the children, they have sent us their lists? We know what they will want?" She huffed. It usually meant that he'd told her already and she hated to be reminded again. "I just want this to be perfect, Mary, my dear. My future niece and my bride to be will be among the guests."

"Yes, I know. I'm sorry, my lord." Oh no, he thought, a *my lord*. He must be in deep trouble. "You should know that I have made you a list and have put it on that mess of a desk you have."

"Have you checked it twice? Trying to find out who is naughty or nice?" She just stared at him, as she usually did when he made a joke that went flat. Duncan tried singing it for her. "You know the song—sing it with me, Mary."

168

"I will not." He'd gotten her goat, as she called it. "What is wrong with you these days? You're acting like a child." She huffed again and muttered all the way back to her kitchen.

Laughing, Duncan made his way to the library. Cowell was there waiting on him, smiling hugely. He asked him if he'd heard them.

"I did. What will you do when she takes a switch to your bottom like she did when you were smaller?" He said he thought he could outrun her now. "You might, but you'll have to return, and she'll be there waiting for you."

"What have you been up to with the computer?" He decided to change the subject. Just thinking of her coming after him with a switch, as she really had when he'd been a child, made him want to limp a bit. "Did you get the revised list that I laid out for you this morning?"

"I did. I have to admit, I never thought of the food for the children. The roast beef and all the trimmings might have been a grand meal for us when we were poor, but I doubt much these children want to have it at a children's Christmas party." Duncan told him how he'd seen a party for children in a book and had gone from there. "Yes. That was brilliant of you. It was easy enough then for you to change it to party favors with a Christmas theme."

"I didn't actually come up with that until I saw some of the paper you'd been ordering to wrap gifts with. That was all on you." Cowell thanked him. "I want this to be an annual thing with the holidays. We'll have something for the children, a little extra cash for the adults to have something nice, and food for them to take home for their own holiday."

Duncan had been at the hospital one morning and one of the nurses told him that there were plenty of children that would go home to a cold house and no food. It was hard, he knew, but he'd never thought of the affect it might have on the little ones in the household. The party and all of it was on Mary.

He'd come home and told her what he'd heard. It hadn't occurred to him that he could help the children, other than giving their parents a gift card for food. She'd smacked him in the back of the head and asked him what he'd have done if he'd only gotten a meal for Christmas and no presents. There were always presents under the tree for him and Cowell, even if it was a sweater that Mary had made them. But he was never hungry; no one was that his mother cared for.

The party was launched that very afternoon, and plans began the very next day to get things set up. The hardest part so far was getting permission for the children to travel to his home. Red tape had nearly killed the idea before it began. And now it was going to happen, and that was where he'd meet his mate.

Chapter 12

Joel stood over the graves of his parents. After they'd been exhumed, he'd asked to have them buried near where he was. The lot at the back of the property that he and Mercy owned was zoned for the purpose, and now he had them close enough that he could go and talk to them, should he wish. Today, he felt, was a good day to see them.

"I wanted you to know how sorry I am that this happened to you. I never thought that he'd do something so cruel as to take you away from me." The bench had been Miley's idea, so he sat down on it after brushing off the newly fallen snow. "He murdered you both. I'm sure you're aware of that, but I wanted to tell you some things you might not have known at the time. Saul thought that there was money, a great deal of it, for some reason."

A small bird landed on the headstone that Piper had made especially for them. It even bore a small picture of them over each of their names, and in the middle, their wedding picture. Every time he looked at it, Joel cried. It was a gift that he never would have gotten without these women in his life.

"I'm married now. I have a wonderful wife. Her name

is Mercy. And Miley is walking now." The bird flew away, and a smallish kitten came to join him on the bench. "Hello there. Where did you come from? My, but you're a pretty little thing."

The kitten mewed at him and he put her down. He wondered if any of the women would object to him having a cat for Miley and laughed. They were birds — they might very well be afraid of it. He'd ask Mercy later if it was still here.

"Saul is going to a federal prison that specializes in handicapped people, such as he is now. I only just figured out that you knew he was a diabetic and that you tried to help him stay on a diet, Mom. But he didn't. In the last month or so he got his levels up so high, and didn't take care of them, that one of his kidneys failed. The doctor that is caring for him said that Saul will not live long. He has given up on trying to be a healthy and better man."

He looked around again, wondering if Saul would be put here with his parents. Then he decided that he didn't want to bury him near here. He hadn't been good to anyone, and he didn't deserve a beautiful resting place.

"I'm going to update you on Saul's health, but I just don't think I'm ready to talk about his behavior about killing off our child. He's lost his leg and the other foot to not caring for himself. And a finger so far. His hands are in bad shape because he refuses to let anyone take care of them. They have to sedate him to get the doctor in to see him. He...well, he throws things at him, fecal matter, and then laughs." Joel cried a little, thinking of the state of his brother. "I wish we could have been a normal family. All I can think of is the day I turned fifteen and him hurting you both so badly, because you'd not let him have the money that Grandma had been sending me all along."

Saul had come into the house just as he was handing his

mom the cash that he'd been sent. Thankfully that was all he'd gotten that day, but Saul had been so pissed off that he beat Mom so badly that she'd ended up in the hospital with nineteen stitches in her head. Dad had had to stay overnight from the concussion that he'd gotten when he'd tried to hold Saul away from Joel. Saul would have more than likely killed him on the spot if not for his dad. As it was, they'd had to use all his money that had been saved to buy prescriptions for them both.

"I never minded that. I know that you felt terrible for it. I could hear you crying that night, and it broke my heart. The money would have been wonderful to have bought something for you and Dad, which was my plan all along, but being able to help you feel better was better than any gift I could have gotten."

Joel sat there for another half hour, not talking about his brother anymore, but he did talk about his life. His new baby coming along, and how well Miley was doing in school. Walking back to his home, he stopped to watch the swans on the lake that hadn't frozen over, and a few deer eating the last of the apples from the trees.

Joel was nearly home when he saw what he thought was a fox kit and remembered the kitten. She was still there when he went back, still curled up under the bench. When he sat down again, picking her up, she mewed at him again and wrapped herself inside of his jacket. He reached out to Mercy to let her know his thinking.

You want to bring a cat into a home of birds. Well, I guess if it didn't mind you, it won't us either. He'd never thought of that and told her. *Yes, well, you've not been a bird as long as I have. A cat might do us some good around here. The barn could use a few of the little beasts to scare away the mice.*

Beasts? I take it at one time you were scared by a cat. She said

173

that it was more than one time, and yes, she didn't much care for the creatures. *But you'll allow this little fella to come live with us? I think that Miley would love a pet of her own.*

Sure, bring her here. But you do realize that Miley could very well be her own pet, don't you? I'm joking, love. Miley has been saying she wanted a pet. I'm just glad she's not asked for anything larger than a puppy. While I'm thinking about it, the horses that you and I wanted are to arrive sometime after the new year. The foals will be big enough to take from Momma then. He told her that was wonderful. *I think so as well. Miley is enjoying her riding lessons now that she's getting around much better. She said that she feels like she's eighty feet tall on the back of a horse. I told her not to fall from that height, or I'll never let her ride again. She laughed, Joel. I don't think she takes me all that seriously.*

She does, but she loves it when you get all mom-like on her. Joel blew kisses to his parents and told them that he'd return soon. Then he made his way, again, back to the house. *I've decided something out here. I don't want Saul to be buried out here with my mom and dad.*

Good. The little fucker needs to be cremated and dumped on a land fill. He would agree with her, but he didn't think he could live with himself if he did that. *I'll see what I can find for the local cemetery. I think we donate the money it takes to clean it up all summer. Maybe they can find us one that no one has purchased as yet.*

I'd like that, I think. I love you, Mercy, and thank you. She said that she loved him too, and to come home. *I'm on my way right now. I have the kitten with me. She seems to like the inside of my coat.*

Because you smell like lunch.

He was still laughing as he came up on the porch. The house was decorated in fall colors now. Miley loved the ability to put out just about anything that she wanted and was having a blast with it. She and Mercy had come home just yesterday with a giant blow up turkey and a pair of pilgrims. Joel was almost afraid of what they'd have for Christmas.

The mailman was just driving up to their mailbox when he sat down on the step. It was just too pretty to be inside. Walking out to get the mail from him, he loved the fact that the man not only knew who he was, but also asked sincerely about Miley.

Taking the mail to the house, he slipped inside with the kitten now in his pocket. Miley came out of the dining room just as he shut the door.

"Mom said that you had something for me. Mail? I didn't send for anything yet." The yet part startled him a little, but she was working and spending her own money. So long as half went into the bank for later in life, then she could pretty much get whatever she wanted. Within reason, of course.

"I do. Here, come and get it out of my pocket while I sort the mail." Having money, he had discovered, meant that you got a great deal of mail daily. Mostly it was people asking for you to give it to them, but sometimes it was just correspondences like the handful he had now. When Miley squealed, he laughed. "I'm guessing that you want her?"

Miley and the cat bonded immediately. The purring of the little cat could be heard all the way across the hallway. When she was asked by Mercy, who had just entered the room, what she was going to call her, Miley didn't even hesitate. She was proclaimed to be Purr. A good name, Joel thought.

"This looks like a wedding invitation. Do we know anyone getting married?" Mercy said that she didn't and took the thick envelope when he handed it to her. "There isn't a return address on it. Isn't there usually one on them?"

"It's not a wedding invitation, but it is an invitation. To a Christmas dinner. It's from—" She looked at him, and he

175

knew that something had upset her. "It's from a man by the name of Duncan Dante."

"Honey, are you all right?" She nodded but sat down. "Mercy, you have to explain this to me before I find this guy and knock the shit out of him for scaring you."

"There is no address for him." She looked up at him, smiling. "It's Dante's son. He's around here someplace. The invitation says that he'll have the address later, for us to join him for a night of fun and games for underprivileged children."

"So, presumably this is when he meets his mate, one of the birds. Do you suppose he knows this? Yes, I would imagine he does. That's why all the cloak and dagger. How long do we have to speculate on who it is?" She told him. "We have six weeks to wait. I'm guessing that we're not going to talk to the others about this? Are they invited as well?"

"Yes, that's why the envelope is so thick. I'm to give one to each of the others. And you're right, I think he does know as much, if not a great deal more than, we do about this." Joel nodded. "And I don't think we should tell any of them. Not yet at any rate. I don't know what they'd do, but I have a feeling that they'd not go. None of them. What I wonder is, if he knows which one of them it is."

"I'd say that if he knows you're all here and that one of you is his mate, then he will know who it is as well." Joel laughed. "I'm not sure I'd want to be in his shoes when he figures out which bird is his, and they find out about all this intrigue going on with it."

"We'll have to make sure that no blood is shed around the kids. After that, it's all up to him." Mercy laughed. "To see Dante's son. It will be such a wonderful thing, don't you think? I mean, it's been so very long. Do you suppose he looks anything like her?"

176

"I would say he must look a great deal like her. I mean, she had some very strong genes, and he would have gotten those, right?" Mercy told him that he'd gotten her magic too. "I bet that he looks like her. It's too bad that there aren't any pictures, or I guess paintings, of her around."

She paused in moving away from him after getting up. "Wait here. I won't be but a little while. Oh, I don't know why I didn't remember this before now. Wait right here." She was her bird, then gone in a matter of seconds, only pausing long enough for him to open the door for her.

Sitting on the porch again, he smiled when he thought of the other birds. Christ, this was going to be epic. She'd be queen. Of whatever was left of the castle, the bird would be queen. Joel thought that was wonderful. That one of Dante's birds would be queen.

~*~

Finding what she was looking for in the dark cave proved to be harder than she thought it should be. Mercy was about to give up when someone cleared their throat behind her. Turning, she knew right away who he was. Bowing low before him, Mercy pledged herself to him.

"I'm not so sure that we need to be doing something like that anymore, Mercy. My goodness, you're much more beautiful up close than you are from a distance. Mother would be so proud of you." Mercy stood, her eyes filled with tears. "Now, let's not have any of that either, shall we?"

"I wondered if you'd look like her. You do. She was my heart for so long, and when the memories began to fade of how she looked, I felt like I'd lost a part of my heart." She asked if she could touch his face. He nodded, and she touched a single finger to his cheek before slapping him. "That's for watching us from a distance instead of making yourself known to us."

"It's the way Mother wanted it." He rubbed his cheek.

177

"You were always so strong. My goodness, how I've missed talking to someone about her. I have Mary still, and her son, Cowell. They knew her, of course, but not as you did, I would imagine."

"Your mother gave her life to save us." Duncan said that he knew that as well; she'd told him of her plan. "I never knew about you until I started reading her books. And I might have missed that too if I'd not taken Latin at some point in my life."

"I don't know her name." She asked him what he meant. "My mate. I know that she is the eagle, but I don't know her name. Can I please ask it of you?"

"Jude. Judith. We call her Jude. Her last name is Castle. We all took some part of the world we had to leave behind as our last names." He sat down on the ornate chair that had been in the castle. "I was looking for her picture. It hung over the fireplace. When your father died, she had one made of just herself to put there. It was a very good likeness of her. Do you have it?"

"No. But I did move it. It was hurtful for me to see it, knowing that I'd never see her again. It's just over there." She walked behind him as he led her to the painting. "I used to think that the smile she had there was for me. But I don't think I was born yet. Do you know?"

"You were born just a mere five months after your father was gone. She took you to Mary to raise, not wanting you to be someone that could be used against her should the castle be taken. Which it never could have been. But by the time we were around, you had already been living with Mary. And to have brought you about after that, it would have frightened a great many people." He nodded, telling her that people would have thought him a fake. "Yes. She took care that no one knew who you were or where you were." She looked at the painting, the memories of her queen hitting her hard in the heart. "Your mother, she was a good person. Hard, but a good person. And she cared a great deal for those that depended on her."

"Yes, I remember that. Even after her death, she took care that everyone was safe." She asked him if he wanted the crown to wear. "No, I don't think so. I understand that your daughter has Mother's. I cannot think of a better place for it to be than with one of her grandchildren. She did think of you all as her daughters, did you know that?"

"No. I mean, she was our maker, so I guess in a way she was our mother too." She moved to stand next to other items that she now wanted to take back with her. "There is a necklace here. It has the image of your mother in it, along with your father. She had put it in the trunk long before we raided the castle for the final days."

"That I have. As well as her wedding dress. I cannot believe that after all this time it was just as beautiful as the day I'm assuming she put it away. I'm going to see if Jude will wear it. What does she do, Jude? I know some of the things that you and the others have done over the years, but not that much about her."

"You should talk to her about things like that. If you know all, then it will not bode well for you when you meet her. I'm assuming that it will be at the party." He nodded and laughed. "I should like to help with that. Not with the plans, but with monies if you'd allow it. I know that you said on the invitation that there was to be an auction, but there has to be something that I can do to help."

"There was once a couple of empty trunks here. If you can find them, then I'd very much like to have those to auction off as well." She said she knew just where they were. "I knew that you would. Thank you. I'll help you get loaded, if you'd like, with the painting. And someday, if you'd not mind, I'd

179

like to have all of you together and someone paint the twelve of us."

"I like that idea. So you think that all the others will find mates as well?" He said that he knew that they would. "I see. And do you know who they are? I don't want you to tell me, but I would like to know that they will be as happy as I am right now."

"Yes, they will all find mates. And Mother knew who they would be. She also knew that Joel would give you her first grandchild." She put her hand over her belly that was just beginning to show a little. "Not that one, although she would have been thrilled for you both, but Miley. Miley is a great addition to the family, Mercy. And I can tell that you love her."

"I do. Very much. Will they all turn to their birds? When Joel and I touched the first time, he became all that I am. Will that happen with the rest of them?" He nodded. "Good. Another thing that I'd like to see for them."

After she was able to put the painting in her pocket by shrinking it a great deal, she found the trunks for him and he took them with him. As she stood in the open field waiting for Duncan to close up the caves, she looked around.

Such a lovely spot here, she thought, and wondered why she'd not thought of putting a nice park here that they could enjoy the view from. As soon as she got home, she was going to talk to Joel about it.

After hugging Duncan and telling him that she was glad to have met him, he begged her not to tell anyone that he was around. Mercy told him that the only person she'd tell was Joel, and that she'd not be able to keep it from him. Smiling, he left her there. Mercy wondered for a moment if he was a bird already, and decided that if she saw him again, she'd ask. Taking flight, she made her way home.

She knew just where she was going to put the painting. It was only fitting that it hung over the fireplace, much like it had in the castle. The sword that Dante had used was hanging with hers, and she knew that it would look good there.

As soon as she arrived home, she noticed the police in the driveway, and went into the house from the rear, coming out the front door just as they were leaving. Joel was sitting on the rocker. She asked him if he was all right and he nodded, then shook his head.

"Saul died this afternoon. They said that he'd been stockpiling his meds and killed himself with a drug overdose. To make sure that he did, they said that he'd taken his monitors off his chest several times the last few days. It was annoying, Allen said, so they just left them off. I guess that was his plan all along." She said she was sorry. "I am too. Not because he's gone, but that I don't have any feelings one way or the other about it."

"He never was a good person. Not just to you, but to anyone that he met." Joel nodded, and she sat on his lap. "I'm so sorry, Joel. I know that he was a pigheaded jerk, but he was your brother."

"He was pigheaded. Allen told me that he'd gone there last week because Saul had called him. Something about the staff trying to keep him from having a good meal. Saul told him that he should take his gun and shoot Miley. That way maybe I'd bring him some cash. Like he needed it where he was headed."

Prison—he had been headed to prison. She'd forgotten about that. Not that he might be going, but the date had been set. The week after Thanksgiving, he would have been going away for good. She wondered if that was what prompted him to hoard his meds.

She took Joel into the house, leading him by the hand

as she might have a small child. Putting the picture on the mantel, they both sat on the couch and looked at it. It was a huge painting, but it was very well done too.

"Most of the time back then, there would have been a hack painting portraits of the royal family. He'd not allow them to see it until he was paid. And even then, he'd make them wait, like maybe picking it up at some other location so that he'd have time to get away." She looked at Joel. "I saw him. Duncan. He was at the cave. But we're not to tell anyone."

"That's wonderful, Mercy. I'm betting that he looks like her, doesn't he? Oh, to have the painting and him in the same place must have been wonderfully revealing." She said that it was, and that he knew who he was mated to. "Let me guess. I'd say Piper. No, not her. She'd eat him alive if he tried this on her. Remi. It's Remi, right?"

"No, Jude. He said that she's his mate and that, just as we guessed, he's going to meet her at the party. And he wishes for her to wear his mother's wedding dress for their wedding. It's been preserved. Dante did that, for him, I think now. My goodness, Joel, he knows a great deal about our future and that of the others."

They talked about the likeness of Dante's painting, and with her face coming back to Mercy, the memory of how beautiful she'd been, other stories about Dante came to light as well. Some she told to Joel, others she left for another time. When he brought up Saul again, she listened while he told stories of the other man.

"I can't think of a single time, not in all our lives, that he was ever kind to someone. You know what I mean. There would be times in most people's life that made them seem as if they were human? Not him. He was a horrible person about everything and everyone." She again told him she was sorry. "Don't be. I know that I should stop talking about him.

But with you, I feel like I can tell you how my heart feels, and you won't judge me about how I feel about him. I was thinking of the reason why he'd never gotten anything from my grandma."

"I would think you'd have to be a pretty bad person for even your grandma not to give you anything for your birthday. I'd like to think that no matter what my grandchild did to me, I'd still want them to have a gift." He said that it wasn't for lack of trying on her part. "What did he do to her?"

"Saul's birthday was in January, just after the holidays, and his card was late coming to him. I was about four or five then. Not too terribly old, but I remember him being so pissed at her. When the card came, two days late, he had a fit. I mean, like he destroyed the mail box and all the mail in it with his fit. Then when he went into the house, Grandma was there, and as I remember now, he picked up a fork that was on the table and stabbed her in the hand with it. It was so bad that it had to be pried from the table." Mercy asked him how he explained himself for such behavior. "He told Grandma that next time she thought to send a card to him, she'd see the scar and remember never to be late again. Then he told her that it would be worse if she was. Grandma stood up and slapped him so hard he fell to the floor, then drew a gun out and pointed it at him as he laid on the floor. I don't know who was more shocked about it, Mom, who was there, or Saul."

"Oh Christ, I wish I could have met her. She sounds like someone that I would have loved." He told her that she'd love her too. "What did she say to the little pisser? I'm sure that it was classic."

"She told him that if he ever drew his hand back to harm her in any way, shape, or form again, she'd come to his bed and blow his head off. Mom told me later that he'd tangled with Grandma before. Then when Saul started to get up, she

183

shot a hole into the floor right between his legs, and told him that next time, she'd not fuck around — yes, she said fuck around — with his twig and berries — they were worth very little anyway — and that she would indeed kill him. After that, there was never a word spoken between them, and he never got another card. Grandma had to have forty-four stitches in her hand. I was both terrified of her and in awe of her at the same time."

Mercy laughed about that several times throughout the rest of the day. She wished she could have met the elderly woman. Mercy would have made her an immortal just to have her around to have fun with. And there wasn't any doubt that they'd have had a blast.

Chapter 13

The funeral was very quiet. No one had shown up but the women and he and Miley. Miley had wanted to stay home, not caring for her uncle, but Mercy talked to her and she was ready to go by the time they were. But she refused to wear black and had worn the most colorful outfit that she could figure out to wear. Joel loved it.

There was no sermon at the graveside. None of them thought that it would have done Saul's soul any good to have had someone pray over him. As they stood there, the grave workers putting the last of the dirt over the casket, he looked around at the place that Mercy had picked out for his brother.

There were no flowers around his grave like the others, and Joel didn't think that there ever would be. The markers at the other sites were old, some of them as old as the town that they lived in. The place, he'd figured out just an hour ago, was for the indigents, as well as prisoners that hadn't any family to claim them. Mercy had been true to her word on finding him a place in the cemetery. It was just as bad as he might have found for him. It wasn't that he hated his brother—he just had no feelings for him. No love, no hatred, just nothing

185

at all. Saul was like a stranger to him.

When the service was over, the last of the dirt piled on his grave, he took a single flower, a daisy that he'd seen in the window at the shop and put it on the grave.

"Maybe you'll get some niceness out of this."

They all walked away, heading to their cars. Mercy had arranged for them to have a nice dinner in town, and then they'd go home to watch an old movie. Even the other birds were going to join them.

He'd not realized how much they all loved popcorn until the other day, when he'd made some. They had eaten six bowls of it before the movie had even begun. It took him several trips to make more before he figured out they were seeds. Laughingly, he made them as much as they wanted, and had purchased a case of it for the next time they came over.

Dinner was at Remi's place. That was what it was called, and the old jukebox had fit well in with the décor she'd come up with. All the stools were covered in red leather, as were the benches, and each table had a small music player at it. Not the old ones—they were very hard to find, not to mention expensive—but new models that entertained as much as the older ones might have.

There were treats after dinner. The malt machine was up and running now. There were apple and cherry turnovers, as well as ice cream that was hand scooped. Everything that a person would need to have a child's, or even an adult's birthday party, Remi told them. To him, it was a perfect ending to the day that they'd had.

"I've been thinking about what you said, Dad, about becoming an attorney. I think I'd be good at that. One for the family. If we're going to be around for a while, we'll need someone to fix the ins and outs of living this long." He told

Miley to do what she wanted. "I am, and I do. I have been looking up on it, and there is a great need for good attorneys. And I want to be the best."

"You will be then." Blaze looked up at him when he laughed. "You don't think she'll be a good attorney?"

"I do. But it's you having so much confidence in her. Just like an aunt would have. I'm very happy that you're going to be there to encourage her along the way." Blaze said that she'd been one once, a good attorney. "Why did you stop doing it?"

"Because, as Miley said, there aren't a great many *good* ones out there. I got fed up with not fighting the system so much as fighting others like me. I hope that she's not getting into it for the money. There are a good deal of people like that as well." Miley asked her if they were all in it for that. "No, I didn't mean to imply that they were only in it for money. But there are a lot of them that are. You have enough money now that it won't be an issue for you, right?"

"No, it won't. I want to be something that I can be proud of. And I think that by being a good attorney, I can be. I mean, not just for the family, though that is a big factor in this. But I'd like to be there for the ones that can't afford a good attorney. That need someone that will fight for them to the very end. That's what I want to do." Joel had never been more proud of her than he was at this moment. "Of course, I might just meet some really nice person and marry him before I can make a go of it."

"No." Joel realized that he'd shouted and lowered his voice. "What I mean is, you're never going to date, marry, or even have a boyfriend."

"Yeah, sure. That's going to happen." Joel glared at Esme. "And that will get you nowhere too. I don't take glares seriously. She'll be and do what she wants. And that, I think, is what we should all want for her. But to say she won't date? You are so a dad if you really think that."

She was right, but that didn't make it any easier for him to think about. Going home, he and Mercy sat on the couch again in the living room, a room that they were both coming to love very much. When Miley said she was going to bed, they both hugged and kissed her then snuggled back into the couch.

They made love there, on the couch, with the fire in the fireplace. Joel removed her clothing as if each piece was priceless. Her skin was touched reverently, as if it might bruise or shatter. His kisses, all over her body, were like tiny brands to her skin, his marking of his mate.

Taking her body, here at this time together, was love. He was sure that this was what the term *making love* came from. It wasn't just a coming together of two bodies. No, it was two souls merging into one. Rolling her to her back, Joel continued to make love to Mercy as he told her with his mouth and voice how much he loved her. That he would cherish her forever, that she was his and only his forever.

And when she came, crying out his name over and over, Joel watched her face, and saw what love she had for him. Kissing her as he released deep inside of her, Joel thought two other people could not love each other as much as he and Mercy. They were one, they were family, and Joel was glad that she'd fallen in love with him.

Life, Joel thought, was very good right now. And as far as he was concerned, it couldn't get any better than it was at this moment.

~*~

Blaze looked over the design that she'd gotten today. It wasn't hard for them to have someone take apart the toys they had — carefully, of course — and then make a diagram of them to use. All the toys had been done that way, except for the few that Miley had helped her with. And they were going to be a big sellers, Blaze thought.

This toy was giving her fits, because the man who had come up with the blueprint for them said that they were perfect and that they moved smoother than Miley had said that they would when she'd been working with her. Blaze didn't see what he might have seen, but she didn't think that it was right. So she took the blueprint and looked it over carefully to find what her mind was telling her was wrong.

After putting it together in her mind, she used a bit of magic and assembled it using just the prints. There was a problem with the movement, but it wasn't the toy's fault, but that of the man who had printed them up for her. He'd left out a very important step.

Picking up the phone, she called him. Deter Prints was going to fix this today for her. As soon as the phone was answered, she knew that something had happened. The person on the other line simply answered the call with "Police."

"Either something has happened to Mr. Deter, or you're there for another reason altogether. Whatever it is, should I be worried about my product?" The man asked her if she was a toy maker. "Yes. I have been in business for a very long time. I inherited the company from my parents."

That was the story that they told anyone they didn't know. It not only explained why the same name held the company, but why it had been in business for so long. Before she could ask again what was going on, a woman came on the line. She was brisk and cold sounding, but efficient.

"What company am I talking to, please?" She wanted to point out that she wasn't a company, but a person, but decided to let it go. For now. "You have a long list of toys that have been made up by Deter Prints, am I correct?"

"He doesn't make the toys for me, but he makes the blueprints for me so that my company can make them. I'm assuming that this is some kind of investigation, and that you have a list in your hand. So, skipping over what you already know, let's get down to business. Why are you there? And why are you going over my list of toys?" Blaze waited for the woman to stop cursing. "Finished?"

"Yes. And you are right, this is an investigation. There were some complaints that toys being made here—or in your case, prints of how the toys needed to be made—were being made by this company, with his name on them. The prints that have gone out, they're not correct, and it's not until they're made that the flaw is found out. Did you find one in the prints you have?"

"Yes, that's why I'm calling. He said they were perfect. And had I put them on the production line like this, I would have had a great many toys that didn't work for me or the people who paid for them." The woman, Agent Williams, asked her if she could come to the plant. "I can. When would be a good time for you?"

"Anytime you can. The sooner the better, if you don't mind." She said that she'd be there in an hour. And she was bringing her attorney. "That might not be such a bad idea. And while you're at it, Blaze, I'd bring anything you have that might tell someone that you've come up with the ideas that you have had him make for you."

This was serious. But she had her ass covered. Blaze or one of them had seen this happen before. Theft of an idea or product wasn't a new thing. And since it wasn't, they'd taken very careful steps in making sure that they came out on top. The next phone call she made was to Jude. She had been the best attorney she knew at one time, and could, at a moment's notice, fall into that position again.

After telling her everything that had happened and what she needed, Jude said that she'd be there in about a half hour. Blaze also told her that she'd drive so that Jude would have time to get her shit together.

"This isn't the first time this has happened to us, so I've been keeping a file ready to grab and go for years. All I have to do is put in the paperwork from Miley's drawings that have been notarized and filed at the courthouse." Jude had been right on top of things for years. And Blaze realized that she didn't think they gave her enough credit for it.

"I don't know what we'd do without you." Jude asked her if she was firing her. "No. Why would you even think that? I was trying to pay you a compliment, dork ass."

"Yes, well, you were doing fine right up until you called me a dork ass. What is that, anyway?" Jude smiled at her. "I love you too, Blaze. And I thank you for the compliment. Maybe when this is over you can take me out to dinner. Or something like that. I've not been out for ages. I mean, like out on a date. How about you?"

"No, there is just too much going on in the world for me to trust people anymore. I know, too, that this isn't the first time for this sort of thing; it all goes in circles. But you just get to the point where you think, fuck it, I've had enough." Jude said that she was the same way. "Though I have to say, I'd love for someone to look at me just one time the way Joel looks at Mercy. It's like he's showing all that he feels for her in a simple glance. You know what I mean?"

"Yes, and when they think they're alone or that no one is looking at them, you could almost feel the heat as it comes off the two of them." Jude leaned back in the seat. "Yes, I'd like for someone to look at me like that too. I'd also take a knight in shining armor to come and sweep me off my feet, take me to his grand castle, and the two of us live there happily ever after. I don't think that happens either, do you?"

"No, sadly I do not. But a castle would be nice. Like the one that we lived in so very long ago. But with a few upgrades. I don't know that I could live without a bathroom or electricity. And the queen, she was so special, don't you think? Like she had all her shit together all the time and nothing upset her. Well, it did, I know that, but she was so graceful about being pissed off."

"Yes, I remember. Once when she was highly pissed at someone—I don't remember the man's name, but he wouldn't surrender his castle, and would let his people starve when she took away his outlet to their farms. But she gathered up what of his people she could, welcomed them to her keep, and then had us crush the castle. It was a good thing that Esme was always able to get in and out to get the staff out. I mean, she was the one with the night vision." Blazed laughed again with her. "This is nice, Blaze. To be together. I miss that."

"I do too, now that I've had a taste of it with you. I think we should get together weekly, the six of us, just so we can talk. Not about work or taking over some business, but just us to get together and go over old times." Jude told her that would be fantastic. "I'm going to get it going too. As soon as we get back, I'm going to pull us all together for a dinner out. I think it will be a blast."

The more she thought about it, the more Blaze loved the idea. This would be a way to get them out of their heads for a little while too. Blaze knew that she was forever thinking of work, what she could be doing if not wherever she was. And having a constant notebook open to jot down more ideas. Yes, she was going to do this. And no cell phones either. Just them, face to face, talking. Blaze wondered how hard it would be to get them to agree just as they were pulling up in front of the building.

"Are you ready for this?" Blaze told Jude that she was. "Me too. We should be done here in no time, don't you think?"

"I think that this will be an all day event that will run into next week. It's never as easy as we hope it will be." Jude got out of the car, agreeing with her. "Please let this be easy. I have shit to do."

Famous last words, she thought.

Before You Go...

HELP AN AUTHOR

write a review

THANK YOU!

Share your voice and help guide other readers to these wonderful books. Even if it's only a line or two your reviews help readers discover the author's books so they can continue creating stories that you'll love. Login to your favorite retailer and leave a review. Thank you.

AWARD WINNING, BESTSELLING AUTHOR

Kathi Barton, winner of the Pinnacle Book Achievement award as well as a best-selling author on Amazon and All Romance books, lives in Nashport, Ohio with her husband Paul. When not creating new worlds and romance, Kathi and her husband enjoy camping and going to auctions. She can also be seen at county fairs with her husband who is an artist and potter.

Her muse, a cross between Jimmy Stewart and Hugh Jackman, brings her stories to life for her readers in a way that has them coming back time and again for more. Her favorite genre is paranormal romance with a great deal of spice. You can visit Kathi online and drop her an email if you'd like. She loves hearing from her fans. aaronskiss@gmail.com.

Follow Kathi on her blog: http://kathisbartonauthor.blogspot.com/

www.ingramcontent.com/pod-product-compliance
Lightning Source LLC
Chambersburg PA
CBHW030223180626
46810CB00008B/2934